The patterns on Foundry Editions' covers have been designed to capture the visual heritage of the Mediterranean. This one is inspired by the architecture of Santiago Calatrava. It was created by Hélène Marchal.

ESTHER GARCÍA LLOVET was born in Málaga in 1963. She moved to Madrid in 1970, where she studied clinical psychology and film direction and has lived ever since. She started writing in 2000 and has written eight novels, including the three novels of her acclaimed Snapshot Trilogy of Madrid (Anagrama). *Spanish Beauty* is the first episode of her new Trilogy of the Spanish Levant. Her works have achieved critical success and cult status for their intense, cinematic style and offbeat Chandleresque realism. García Llovet writes for several different cultural anthologies and periodicals, as well as being a translator from English and a well-respected photographer.

RICHARD VILLAGE is a London-based translator and editor working from Spanish and Italian into English. He studied literary translation at the University of East Anglia and is the founder of Foundry Editions.

SPANISH BEAUTY

ESTHER GARCÍA LLOVET

Spanish Beauty

Translation by Richard Village

**FOUNDRY
EDITIONS**

Para mi madre, siempre aquí

A solitary two-seater chair, lit from above by a spotlight, surrounded by the blackest, most impenetrable darkness. It's impossible to love so few people, but he knew that he just couldn't help it. His new heart had foretold the worst, and the prediction had come true.

KIKO AMAT, *REVANCHA*

A glow glimmering like some interstellar advert out in the middle of the ocean, at the end of a night at the end of summer. The dry glow of a cigarette. It crackles into life, goes out, burns again in the bow of the Zodiac. She smokes and talks at the same time, alone. Then she calls someone on her phone. A few minutes go by. She chucks the cigarette into the water. It sinks, hissing. Directly beneath the Pole Star. Lime green reflection on the acid sea; five in the morning, the shittiest time of day, the turnstile to the other side.

Electronic sky.

The letters: red. And square: Benidorm.

Now that dawn is breaking, everything stays in its place. The full moon stays in its place, transparent, porous, like chalk. The dinghy slowly approaches Finestrat beach like a basking shark scoping the surface of the sea. Michela stands in the bow. She has the look of someone who hasn't slept a wink so they can wake the world up; damp and cold, her usual look, her hair stiff, hardened with salt. When she reaches the shore, she turns off the engine, jumps into the water, drags the Zodiac a few metres and dumps it there on the sand. She's in jeans, a crocheted bikini top, her boots hanging round her neck by their laces. She walks up the flat beach. She passes a couple sleeping off the night before, a dog rooting around in some Lidl bags, the remains of a bonfire put out with beer. She heads for the beach bar where the music is coming from. It's something by C. Tangana, playing in stereo from some cheap plastic speakers hanging over the heads of a couple having beer for breakfast and reading *The Sun*. Sandals, white socks, yellow gold signet ring on the little finger; that's him. She's in a wheelchair, ankles like church candles, emerald-green eyeliner, taking photos of the dawn with her phone.

"No photos or videos, madam," Michela tells her. Michela speaks impossible cockney, like she's Hackney born and bred.

"Who are you, anyway?"

"Where's Martin?" Michela asks the waiter.

In the bar, the chairs are still on the tables, except the one the English are at. It smells of frying, of coffee, of sun oil.

"Martin's having a few days off." The waiter has the same accent as Michela even though he's never set foot in London in his life. Or anywhere outside Benidorm.

"Then you and I can party. It's his birthday," she tells the Englishwoman.

"Happy birthday," says the Englishwoman and takes his photo.

"It's not my birthday. I'm working. Anything else?" he asks the English couple.

"For you two to shut it," says the man.

"I've got a surprise for you," Michela tells the waiter.

"I don't like surprises."

Michela bursts out laughing.

"Says who."

"Says me," says the Englishman.

Michela picks up a chair and sits looking out to sea.

"I'll have a coffee. Where's he gone? I've been looking for him for three days."

"Not a clue," says the waiter, taking the chairs down from a table. He's wearing a girl's apron. "Leave me out of your dramas."

"Today's not a day to be wasting time," says Michela. "It's never a day to be wasting time, especially not here. Here, everyone goes around as if they had all the time in the world: they do nothing, they go brown, they eat and get pissed, not a clue that time's all they've got, there's nothing else, all that bollocks about if you don't use your head some-one will use it for you is complete shit. What you've got to do is use other people's time for what you need, for what you want. Use it, own it, see what happens."

"I don't go brown," says the woman.

"Right here, right now, everyone's gone soft. Nothing happens, nobody wants anything, and that's the worst thing that can happen. Stupid and boring. Leftovers and fag ends. And this bastard sun."

"What do you mean boring?" She's in a dress with sun-flowers on it, though she must be seventy if she's a day. "This place is the biggest laugh in the world."

"The Russians are saying it's a laugh too," says her husband, reading the paper. "It's in here."

"Which Russians?"

"The ones who've bought the big house at Terra Mítica," he smiles. He's got a brand-new set of teeth. "They're having a housewarming."

The waiter heads over to the coffee machine. He makes a thick black one, no sugar. When he gets back, Michela has gone. She's left her cigarettes on the chair, gone back to the shore, got into the Zodiac. Michela pulls the starter. One, two, three. It starts, the engine turns over a couple of times a few metres out until it settles down. Then she points towards the horizon. The Englishman asks for his third pint of the morning.

"Your dealer's a piece of work," he tells the waiter.

"She's not my dealer."

"Come off it. I saw you give her an envelope under the table."

The waiter sits at one of the tables and sips the coffee. Then he throws the paper cup on the floor and listens to the frothing waves breaking on the shore. He lights a cigarette.

"She's not my dealer. That's Michela. She's police."

Michela speeds up, stands on the bow, and takes off, leaving a strong smell of petrol and a narrowing wake of whipped-up foam, a line of coke disappearing off out to sea like a liquid motorway, thin and faint, straight towards the warm moon. Deep speed. Sunday.

Benidorm. Cheap culture. Beach culture. People who speak three languages without ever studying, corner shops, Belgians, watered-down gin and tonics, gays. Second-hand Tom Clancy novels, swollen with damp, crunchy with sand, sand on your pillow, sand in your paella, in your G-string, in the shower, all-day fry-ups, all-day Thai massage, cicadas at night. Piles of sick, pissing against walls, and Tom Jones songs. Melanomas, cystitis, diarrhoea all round. Chlamydia. And the sea. Like the desert of the Levant, of the West, of Las Vegas, shadows of skyscrapers on the beach, reaching higher and higher, shadows that go on for miles, stretching over the surface of the lukewarm sea at ten at night whilst families eat fried chicken on the shore, Mediterranean steel Godzillas on the cold dawn sand.

Martin lives in an Airbnb. In a nine-euro-a-night room, in a tiny villa in Rincón de Loix behind the endless row of nine-euro-a-person Chinese buffets. The room has two beds, he uses one for sleeping and the other as a kind of table where he eats, writes his songs, and leaves his things. Not that he's got much. Dirty T-shirts and Alan Moore comics. There's a photo pinned to the wall, a postcard of some compact white clouds and, beneath each one, some blocks of ice floating on a grey ocean, like exact reflections of the clouds. The postcard is from Canada. It says so underneath. Canada. There's also a White Stripes poster.

"Where the fuck are you?" growls Michela. She opens the drawer on the bedside table. It's lined with floral vinyl. Empty. Ants. There's only one plug in the room and if Martin wants to turn on the water heater to wash or to charge his phone, he has to unplug the lamp and do it in the dark. The phone charger is plugged in. So, Martin hasn't gone anywhere, or won't have gone far, he's almost definitely in Benidorm. Where, is the question. Michela picks up a pair of jeans from the bed and checks the pockets. She finds a receipt from the Multipollo chicken shop at the bus station. She looks at the date. It's from 11.47. 11.47 this morning.

"Martin's not here and I don't know when he'll be back," Oliver answers.

Oliver is one of her better informers, a youth in a hoodie who thinks he's much smarter than he actually is, though Michela wouldn't dream of telling him because his I've-seen-it-all-before bullshit works for her. He's sitting in one of the four black leather massage chairs at the end of the walkway in the bus station shopping centre. They look like the ones pilots practise in and never work. The glare from the skylight above the central hall is fierce and dusty.

"You're going to tell him that he either answers my call or he steers clear of Benidorm. For good."

"He's taken three days off, that's all I know." Today Oliver's got a shaved eyebrow. He'll have seen it on Netflix.

"Just tell him to pick up his phone. Got it, fuckwit."

Oliver puts his hands in the pouch of his hoodie and scratches his crotch.

"Is he ghosting you? Don't get desperate, it's not a good look on you."

Michela puts her hands on the back of the chair and eye-balls Oliver.

"Call him right now. In front of me."

"My phone's been nicked," Oliver laughs.

"Don't give me that shit."

Oliver lifts his arms, as if to say "go for it". Michela frisks him and it's true; it's not in his hoodie or his jeans. He doesn't even have house keys. She pulls away.

"Speak to him and tell him to ring me or to come to my place. Today. Tonight. Now move it before I boot you out of here."

Oliver nods, reluctantly gets up, goes off down the corridor scraping his flip-flops on the floor, and leaves through the chicken shop, where a dozen birds are slowly turning, a spit up their arses, burnt, stiff, dead, headless.

Sea by day, sea by night. Sky the colour of Fanta by day and at the dead of night, the Milky Way, Venus, constellations looping like motorway junctions and maps of lost highways against the deepest black. Out at sea, about three kilometres from the coast, you can hardly see Benidorm, except for the odd light from the highest skyscrapers, glints appearing and disappearing behind the stealthy, catlike waves. They finished the jet-ski race just a few moments ago and they've already switched off the engines. Tonight's was quicker than usual, an Italian won, an entrepreneur from Milan, barely twenty, never out of his wetsuit even when he's on the cover of magazines, and now all seven competitors have gathered round Michela's boat and are standing on their jet-skis. Some are smoking, others are checking their phones, downing cans of booze. A girl, no bikini, proper skinful, flings herself into the water. The Italian is counting the winnings he's just got his hands on but absolutely doesn't need. The money comes in a roll, tied up tight with a hairband, many more notes than if the races were legal and out in the open. Like everything done in secret, it's a hefty sum, though what you pay an arm and a leg for isn't always worth it. Michela is sitting in the back of her boat, in the darkest part where nobody can see her, making sure everything is running smoothly, that none of these brats who have come from Ibiza or Marseille get silly because they've lost and spoil this little set-up she's been running for the last five summers. She takes fifteen per cent. She could take much more but she doesn't need it. She really does it because she finds out a thousand and one things that are going on, every little scam, who's doing what to whom. The boys from Ibiza are talking about getting 2C-B for the Russian party, they're laughing non-stop like they're already on it, which they probably are. One jumps into the water and starts to swim away from the jet-skis. He's singing "Azzurro". When he gets about a hundred metres away, he starts to shout for help. Nobody pays any attention, they ignore him, his timing is off for the adrenaline rush they all need at least three times an hour. Michela gets a message. It's from Martin.

What do you want. That's all he's written.

She messages back. Some Russians are having a party and are looking for a band.

When can we meet up.

Tomorrow afternoon my house.

Okay.

Michela. Michela McKay. The door to the landing with the lift was open, but the flat was dark. She left the light off as she went in. She'd heard the call from the station on the patrol car radio whilst her partner Vilches was buying cigarettes, a call about fighting in a flat on the Playa Poniente. When he came back, she didn't mention it because she wanted to go up by herself, on her own terms, without Vilches and his potato face. So, leaving him in the dark, she went up the twelve floors and into the flat, in the dark. Bare yellow walls, rental-flat pine furnishings, a huge sitting room where she stopped and stood completely still, like another piece of furniture. There wasn't a sound. Just the gentle hum of the microwave in the open-plan kitchen, its square, orange light on the sitting room's terrazzo floor. Michela put her hand on the pistol in her belt and slipped through the flat like the shadow of a ghost's shadow. She made her way to the bedroom. Some light was coming in from the window. There was nobody there, the bed was made, and the things you expect from a bedroom were all in the right place. Bathroom: nobody, nothing. Not even a drip from one of the taps. She went back to the sitting room. She opened the cupboards. Some Amazon boxes, empty, a pair of flip-flops. She slowly turned her head to one side then the other. Her hand ached from squeezing her pistol. She breathed deeply. The only thing working was the microwave. Turning and turning and that hiss, intense but distant at the same time. She went up to look. There was something inside. She didn't recognise what it was until the plate went round again and she could see it from the front: two hands. Two hands, one on top of the other, no ring, like a pose from a Renaissance portrait, completely burnt and slowly turning on their small, circular stage. Blackened. A woman's hands.

The woman's body never turned up, in Benidorm or anywhere else. Neither did the owner of the flat. A couple of months later, without anybody mentioning anything, Michela ended up moving in and living there. It's a very quiet flat, almost hidden at the end of a corridor on the twelfth floor of the building next to the Hotel Lido, the one with all the creepers growing up it.

Martin is sitting at the bar, which doubles as a kitchen table, waiting for her. Martin has no idea about the hands. He has no idea about lots of other things to do with Michela.

"Your plants have all dried up," says Martin.

"That's what happens. What's that?" she says, pointing to a box by the front door. "Have you brought me a present?"

"They dropped it off a while ago."

"Who?"

"I don't know. Someone. He had a helmet on."

"Don't open the door. Never open the door to this flat. Especially if I'm not here."

"But you're never here."

Michela goes to the kitchen, opens the fridge, takes out a Tupperware of fried rice. The fridge is where the microwave used to be. There's a lot of Tupperware in the fridge, stacked up like samples in a forensics lab.

"What's this about a party then?"

"It's a housewarming. Some Russians are throwing it for the big place they've just bought."

"The one in Terra Mítica?"

"That one. Now they're looking for a band."

"What's their story?"

"There are seven brothers. I think the whole clan is flying in on some private jet of theirs. The Brothers Kaminski. Each one has got seven sons as well. Sounds like the beginning of a joke but it isn't, and they're all identical, a whole legion of Russians. They all dress like each other too, just to make things even more confusing. I'm not sure how it's going to work when they get here, if they're all moving in, but they must be because they've bought that whole massive villa with fifty rooms, and they already speak Spanish. The sons already speak Spanish, the language of the future. Mind you, there are so many of them, they could invent a new language and just take it with them wherever they go, like all the Russians do."

"Have you been drinking?"

"What I like most about the Kaminskis is how well they've done everything. No, I've not been drinking. I'm taking the piss. There are three brothers, that's all. The father started out with a security alarm business, small stuff, nothing to write home about. Not a big success, mainly because there were hardly any break-ins where they lived, it was a bit out of the way like El Saler and Valencia, nothing going on. It was a holiday place, and half the houses were empty over the winter. Old man Kaminski had the great idea to get his sons to trash the houses a bit, stage the odd break-in, smash a window, swipe what was there, genius stuff like that so that the neighbours would get their act together and get an alarm. And they got their acts together. It all worked like a dream, now they just do alarms, they've invented some new system and made a fortune, so they want to come over here and spend it all. I think it's great, they love the sun. All gloomy Russians are the same, but happy Russians want to have fun in their own way. And no, I haven't been drinking, but I could do with one. Want something?"

"What I want is to go home soon. We're going to Barcelona tomorrow to the Eels concert and we've got to leave early."

"The ones you've got the T-shirt of?"

Martin always wears a yellow T-shirt with Mr E's face on it.

"Them."

"They're playing in Valencia. I've seen the posters."

"I know, but I want to go to Barcelona."

There are four of them in Martin's band. Four handsome twenty-somethings who are neither good nor bad but try hard. Martin's band is called Foneda Cox, after the boxer, because one of them reads fanzines and comics from Valencia, which are the best in Spain. At weekends, they play on the roof terrace of a hotel five blocks back from the beach, or at the flea market and, if they get lucky, they get called for private parties. Sometimes they get a gig outside Benidorm, weddings in Albacete. They have a podcast, and they want to release a record, but in truth they don't make a penny. Sometimes they hang out with a bunch of graffiti artists who make "interventions" on whole façades of buildings and spray anti-establishment messages over the walls of Benidorm. Like this was Europe. When Michela hears words like "anti-establishment" or "intervention", she gets twitchy. They've got lots of ideas but may as well have none. Playing at one of the big fiestas, being on some TV competition or the support act in one of the thousands of summer festivals, that's what they want. To play for the Russians.

"They know all the right people," says Michela, "in Russia. I'm going to make you a Negroni."

"No."

"Then have a beer."

"How many people are going to be at this party? What day's it on?"

"Next Saturday." Michela goes to the built-in bar, makes her drink, and gets out a can of beer. She puts the can in front of Martin. "I'm going to ask you a favour. Actually, it's not a favour."

Martin looks at her. "I'm not interested."

"You don't even know what it is yet."

"But I know you and I know what you're like."

Michela takes a sip of her Negroni. She puts an ice cube in her mouth. She savours the taste of it and then spits it slowly back into the glass.

"You just have to pinch a lighter."

"A lighter?"

"Reggie Kray's lighter."

"Reggie Kray's lighter. You're not still going on about that?"

Reggie Kray. Ronnie and Reggie, the Kray Twins, The Firm. Threats, extortion, arson, robbery, bribery, murders in broad daylight, always that swagger, winkle-pickers, thick-rimmed glasses, a cigarette. They swanned around the pubs of the East End, dressed up like Michael Caine: fitted jacket, narrow tie, gold signet ring on the little finger, walking slowly, carefully, the way well-built people do in expensive clothes, so as not to tear them, all before they ended up with chunky, boxers' bodies in the most squalid prisons in the country, Shepton Mallet and the Tower of London, for murdering a member of a rival gang.

"Incredible, right?" Michela smiles. "After all this time. The Russian bought the lighter at an auction two years ago. I've been trying to track it down ever since and now it's going to be here. Right here in Benidorm. At that party."

"Why don't you ask Oliver or the German?"

"Because they're morons."

"You think everyone's a moron."

"Everyone except you."

Martin downs his beer and holds up his palm, as if ending a conversation he's been having with himself.

"Do you think I'm a fuckwit, or what. If you're not asking Oliver, it's because the whole thing is more fucked up than you're letting on."

"It'll be as easy as the thing with those German women at the airport."

"I've got better things to do."

"You're missing the opportunity of a lifetime."

Martin goes towards the front door of the flat.

"You've locked it," he says, holding the handle.

"And swallowed the key."

"Open the door."

"You don't get it, do you."

"I totally get it and I'm not bothered if I don't get the gig."

Martin goes across the sitting room and opens the terrace window. The flat is the last one on the floor and there's scarcely a metre between the terrace, where Michela keeps an exercise bike that she doesn't use and an equally redundant barbecue, and the fire escape. There's a pool below where some boy killed himself a couple of summers back by throwing himself into the water from the third-floor balcony. Someone in his family has tied a bunch of plastic flowers to a lamp post.

"Such a drama queen," says Michela, but she doesn't get up from the bar. Behind her, there's a poster of *Alfie*, which she saw a thousand times when she lived with her father.

"Open the door."

"When have you ever played in front of a thousand people."

"I will do."

"God you're a pain in the arse. All you've got to do is get the lighter off him, he's always carrying it around, it brings him luck. I've seen it in thousands of photos. It won't even take a minute."

"Give me the keys."

"You aren't listening. You're just saying no for the sake of it. It's a rubbish argument. It's a loser's argument."

"Give me the keys. Seriously."

Michela shrugs her shoulders. She throws him the keys.

"You're more of a pain in the arse."

Benidorm, the city that never sleeps, the city in every time zone at once, the city where the bars are open till the day after tomorrow. The Casino Mediterráneo's opening hours don't matter, because, like all casinos, it has no windows, no views to the outside world, so you have no idea if it's daytime, night-time, or whatever. The casino is on the edge of Rincón de Loix, midnight-blue glass, an enormous neon palm tree shining on the avenue side of the façade and a little path where the usual types who loiter about casino car parks hang out: old loan sharks, runners with all the time in the world, girlfriends with bags under their eyes, darker, deeper, and more terrifying than their impending ruin.

El Potro is sitting on a motorbike that isn't his but looks as if it is. El Potro looks twenty years younger than the fifty he actually is. El Potro's speciality is pawning Rolexes and BMWs and wedding rings for gamblers that leave at three in the morning in a state, with pale green faces and fever running high, after they've lost everything but are still up for losing more. They'll always find El Potro waiting to look after them. El Potro is listening to music and rolling a fag.

"It's been a while, Michela."

"Get your headphones off."

"You what?"

Michela takes his headphones off herself.

"I was saying that all songs are different, but silence is always the same."

"What can I do for you, sweetheart."

"Have you seen this bloke hanging about?"

Michela takes out her phone and shows him the picture of Kaminski. In one of his characteristic moments of productivity and clear thinking, moments so rare and brilliant that they clear a month's worth of paperwork in five minutes, it was Vilches who had passed on the information that Kaminski was into poker, roulette, gambling, and so on. Like all Russians. Afterwards, he had gone back to sleep on his desk in the police station. Vilches is one of those policemen who went into the force with absolute faith in law and order. First, he lost faith in the law, then he lost faith in order, and then moved straight on to third-generation inhibitor antidepressants. Sometimes, one or two afternoons a week when he wakes up from his four-hour siesta, he puts in an appearance at the station. The rest of the time, not.

El Potro takes Michela's phone. He spends a couple of seconds looking at the photo.

"No, gorgeous."

"Are you sure? Have another look."

El Potro shakes his head. Michela trusts him, they know each other, they had a bit of a moment years ago that neither of them can remember. Which is a good thing.

"Okay," says Michela, "let me know if you see him."

"Are you off? Don't you fancy a little something?"

"I haven't got time."

"Off you go to run over old ladies, then."

Michela heads off to the avenue; it's true that she hasn't got time, but she's always got the urge.

"Tell Kyle I owe him a round!" shouts El Potro after her.

Michela stops in her tracks. "My father's in Benidorm?"

"He's been here for a month. Hasn't he? More or less. You'll know better than me."

"Right."

"Call him and tell him I'll see him tomorrow."

Michela nods. She crosses the avenue, eyes fixed on the zebra crossing, which suddenly looks like a flight of stairs that could trip her up at any minute. Her father is in Benidorm. She'd call him if she knew his number. He's never given it to her.

She thinks better when she's driving. When she thinks she has to talk, very quickly, without drawing breath, and very loudly until she ends up working out what's in her head. Then she can get out of the car and finally shut up. She was signed up to BlaBlaCar for a couple of years, doing the old Madrid–Valencia clubbing route several times a week, just to talk to someone who didn't know her and sort out her problems. The minute she got to Madrid, she'd turn straight back because the capital? No interest at all. One afternoon, though, she did make it to the Bernabéu, which she thought looked like the most elegant-ugly, expensive high-security prison in the world. Michela also discovered that BlaBlaCar was much better than Tinder, no strings and plenty of motels the whole way along the A3. You even got your petrol paid for. She had the odd nocturnal encounter, nothing major, and then gave it up. Now she takes the patrol car when it's available. It's more comfortable. Cheaper. More boring.

She picked the kid up a while ago, at the top of the dirt track that leads to some next-big-thing, many-starred restaurant. He'd put a chain across the track, barring the way, and was charging guests two euros to get through as they arrived. Michela was sure about him the minute she discovered him sitting there under a parasol, plugged into

33

Spotify with a chain hitched between two palm trees in the forty-degree heat. She'd easily be able to sneak him into Kaminski's party and he'd definitely be handy with his fingers. Bung him a cool hundred and see you never. She put him in the back seat. He's a short-arse, and she has to move the rear-view mirror down to see his face.

"What was your name?"

"You've already seen it on my ID."

Not an idiot. He's got her number quickly.

"That's not an answer. And it's you've seen it on my ID, *Officer*."

"Arturo. Are we going to the station? Because this isn't the way."

"We're going to see what happens."

Arturo must be in his twenties but looks about forty. Michela checks him out in the mirror, working out whether he'll do for what she needs, whether he's got just the right level of fear, not too much and not too little.

"Can I see your badge, Officer?" Arturo asks her.

"No."

"Where's your partner, Officer?"

"At the bottom of the sea. For asking too many questions."

"I want to see your badge. I've got my rights, Officer."

Michela takes her pistol out of her belt and lays it on top of the glove compartment.

"Here's my badge."

Arturo looks away and stares out of the window. They're leaving Benidorm: right now, they're in that no man's land where adverts stay for five years without being changed; peeling, pale blue, frazzled by the sun.

"What do you want?"

Arturo looks at her in the rear-view mirror.

"I want to have a laugh with the Russians. We have to have a laugh with the Russians, right, because the Russians know all about laughs. Vodka, polonium-210, and a stray dog in space. Who can top that? They never go brown, so they come here, to Spain, to our bottled flamenco sun, and we can't get our heads round why. To buy flats, apartment blocks on the beach, the biggest mansion on the whole Costa de la Luz, a villa with acres of land around it, a Mediterranean pine forest and a golf course with a president chucked in. We see them, all these Russians, in the clubs, in cars, in the restaurants in packs of six or seven. The French and the English, sometimes you see a lone one on the loose, but never a Russian. You only ever see lone Russians lurking around the doorways of five-star hotels, neither in nor out, as if they can't make up their minds, but they know exactly what they want. They want Spanish hedonism. Dionysian hedonism that only the tourists and the travel agents get to see, because the reality here is that we're always really pissed off, and really burnt, not just by the sun. The Russians want the hedonism we don't get to enjoy, they want the prices we can't afford, they want the siesta we can't even take. And they want music, music all night long. Benidorm! Fiesta!"

"Hundred per cent."

"What would you know."

Arturo touches the chain around his neck and pulls out a cross, an enormous Orthodox cross the size of a fist, like a rapper's medallion.

"A Russian gave me this. What do you reckon?"

"I reckon it's alright."

"It's got the Nike logo on it. A crucifix with Nike on it. They've been around for like, a thousand years, these crosses, and now they've branded them. They're so, like, modern, the Russians. And the Chinese, way more."

"Where did you pinch it?"

"I didn't pinch it. I got given it."

"Who by?"

"Some guy called Kaminski."

Michela snarls. Kaminski. For fuck's sake, they've only just got here and they're already everywhere. Too risky: this kid could report back to him the minute he gets out of the car. She slows down. She pulls over to the side of the road and stops the patrol car. She unlocks the door.

"Out. Piss off. I'm bored of you."

Arturo gets out of the car.

"Later, Officer."

Handsome thugs, like you get in films, do exist, but ugly ones are much more effective: they only have one way to release the inner anger they feel because they're ugly. Back in Leeds, Rob had been one of those, skinny and ugly; but before coming to Benidorm, he'd had his face fixed with all the cash he'd earned over the past fifty years from one smooth face-smashing after another. He'd kept the bad blood, though, getting darker and more putrid as time went on, as well as a reputation for unshakeable loyalty and crazy, unexpected obsessions that were always over before they began.

"Stop with all your sodding stupid stories," says Rob with a lisp. There'd been no fixing that. Rob is sitting right at the back of a pub with photos of the Queen Mother everywhere and a huge top-quality, acorn-fed ibérico behind the bar. It's seven in the evening. Or nine in the morning.

"But it's a family thing," says Michela.

"It's your family thing," Rob interrupts, pointing at her with his stubbed-out cigarette. "We've all got our own, Mike."

"Family, mis cojones." That's Winnie, Rob's wife. She says things in Spanish. Winnie is a blonde, about thirty, widowed three times, arched eyebrows drawn on because the real ones have been shaved off.

She's right.

"Kaminski's a free agent. He's not in a gang. He's just got some cousins, that's it. He's here to do business. His hands are clean," says Michela.

Rob lifts his index finger to his forehead as if to say that the Russians think differently or are mad or something.

"You'll find out what you're getting yourself into, Mike."

The Mediterranean franchise of the Grant Gang of Leeds is officially made up of three people – Rob, Winnie and their brother-in-law – plus seven or eight interchange-able, nameless relatives who could equally well crop up in Leeds, Benidorm, or La Línea de la Concepción. It was the Grants who sorted it for Michela to get into the police, a win for all of them, a fifty–fifty split that's worked for fif-teen years like a fixed pinball machine: Michela gets total protection inside the force and the Grants have a foot in the National Police. Everyone happy as Larry. And it has to be said, no one's ever touched a hair on Michela's head. For this spring/summer season, the Grants have gone deep into the tourism sector and slipped a kilo of coke onto every Leeds–Benidorm flight. Red Samsonite with a green strap. Michela at Customs. 18.15 flight. To travel! To leave coun-tries behind! And suitcases.

Michela looks at Rob. She could threaten him with leav-ing her post at Border Control if he doesn't help her out, but no one threatens this lot. There's no way to convince them, apparently. She doesn't get it. After all, Reggie Kray's lighter has become a talisman, a legend, an amulet, the ring from Lord of the Rings for whoever its owner might be, the Ring of Power.

Winnie gets up, sixteen stone or thereabouts, pastel-painted toenails, and goes to the bar. She brings over three cans of beer and sits back down next to Rob.

"Forget the whole thing, Mike."

In the bar, two hundred square metres if not more, there's not another soul.

The ficus in the garden has grown back wilder and more uncontrolled than she remembered as a child, the brooding, ever-present guardian of the false myth of the family home, casting a deep shadow on the empty pool with its geological strata of rotten leaves, fag butts, and condoms. Michela can't stand coming here, to her neighbourhood, to her house. She hasn't for years. She finds the keys on her MacGyver key ring. When she opens the door, all the stuff is suddenly in her face. It's freezing inside. The corduroy curtains have been drawn for a thousand years, nobody has touched anything for an age, and it's covered with the fuzz of ancient dust, very picturesque, very European. Very un-Benidorm. She stands in the middle of the sitting room, like she's on stage in a play that's ended. Badly. There's the record player next to the sofa the colour of gas canisters, her mother's vinyls, hundreds of Kyle's books. From the sitting room she can see the feet of her parents' bed, its indigo sheets, why do ghosts always have sheets, she suddenly thinks, as if the spirit grabs the first thing it comes across before leaving and that's the fabric covering it. She heads into the corridor. At the end, there's the poster of the Kray Twins. Life-size. They're in fitted jackets, narrow ties, black glasses, the best-looking boys in the neighbourhood, in the whole of the East End, which is laid out in the picture behind their beefy shoulders: Spitalfields, Whitechapel, Shoreditch before it was Shoreditch. Patent leather lace-ups. No one dresses like that any more. Ronnie and Reggie Kray, "your London uncles", Kyle used to say, something she took literally for far too long, something she might still believe.

Michela goes back to the sitting room. With the end of a biro, she lifts up some magazines, some of the stuff, clothing, as if they were evidence in a murder case and she mustn't leave any fingerprints. There are papers, press cuttings, Kyle's interview with the last prisoner from the Maze. Underneath it all, there's the Nagra tape recorder that he recorded the interviews for his book on. The recordings. The interview with Terry B., Reggie Kray's cellmate, third-rate delinquent and Tube station pickpocket, who ended up living in Benidorm and was what had brought Kyle here to the Pearl of the Costa Blanca in the Olympic year, 1976.

Kyle and Terry B. got to know each other one April in the Mars, a bar on one of the flights of steps in the old town. Terry B. was small and wiry, low-maintenance, one of those people who eats once a day and sleeps one night a week. When he was drunk, he told stories about Reggie. When he was sober too. It was his big topic, his life's mission. It justified his place in the world. His interview with Kyle went on for days, Terry B. even telling him how Reggie used to talk in his sleep, about the terrible poems he wrote on paper napkins, how he'd wake up calling for his mother, during the long, silent nights in jail. Yes, the interview went on for days, at Terry B.'s house, a tiny flat, half a square metre with the blind always down and the light always on. He was stony broke, he didn't have a penny left from the old days, he'd blown it all on blow and blowing the rent boy at the Mars. On the last night, after four nights of interviewing, Terry B. offered Kyle Reggie's lighter. He offered to sell it for peanuts so he could survive till the end of the month, so he could go out on the floats for Holy Week. Kyle bought it without a second thought. In exchange Terry asked him to say nice things about him in the book, to skip over the drugs stuff. To make him look good, know what I mean. Reggie Kray's lighter for five hundred pesetas. That's how they left it. "The happiest day of my life." That's what Kyle said to Michela many years afterwards. Many years after it had been stolen too.

Michela leaves the Nagra tape recorder where it was, under all the papers for Kyle's book: *The Seven Crowns*, a comparative study of Shakespeare's regicide plays and the London underworld gangs of the fifties. He never finished it. Next to an ashtray full of cigarette butts, there's a photo of her father, of Kyle, sitting in a garden at Eton, his shadow as extensive as his fortune. A couple of years back, Michela had to go on a trip to England, to London. She was only there for three days, for work, investigating an English doctor falsely diagnosing food poisoning for his fellow countrymen, one of the many scams that had added yet more polish to the golden name of Benidorm. She stayed in Whitechapel, where else. She liked the sky the colour of boiled cod, how friendly the locals were, almost like country people, the unshowy affluence everywhere that seemed made for the over-fifties, the accumulation of wealth. She had one free afternoon. She went to see the Tower of London, on the lookout for the ghosts of her ancestors and the prophetic ravens, and she found both. Everything in London, she thought, feels as if it's been used twice, once by history and once by the people themselves, and she wondered what it would take for history to become so all-encompassing in a place like Benidorm, whether twelve-month-long holidays, week-long drinking binges and bone idleness twenty-four hours a day could ever add up to anything you might call a historical event, a revolution, a climax, a conquest. She thought not. In Benidorm ambitions are in line with the small scale of the crime: half-arsed drug dealing, scams, punch-ups. Get-rich-quick urban development and sleazy local politics if you want to think big. Nothing else. That's all we've got. We don't make history any longer. We make sangria.

Michela scans the place, looking for something that might be a clue to whether her father has been there recently, something that might tell her who he is these days, but the T-shirt and the typewriter, which look like the only recent additions, tell her nothing. Or maybe it's that people only rub off on things when we remember them together, and now she barely has any memories left of Kyle. Or maybe they aren't speaking to her because there seems to be no deliberate choice behind them, because the person behind them cares as little for things as he does for people. When she leaves, she triple-locks the door. Then she goes to the San Remo and downs four yzaguirres. After that, she gets up and spends the rest of the afternoon fining any vehicle that crosses her path.

Martin has been to buy a couple of twelve-packs of beer and Coke and has planted himself on the main road out to the A3, at the last traffic lights coming out of Benidorm before the motorway. It's Sunday and day trippers on their way home will buy anything for their journey. He could sell stuff on the beach too, but out here sometimes, in his head, he sees himself leaping into one of the cars and heading off into the distance towards the myth of Barcelona, or Berlin, or anything Cool with a capital C, and leaving all this behind. Swapping the skyscrapers for gothic cathedrals and hotel pubs for the Razzmatazz. He nearly always sells the lot in under half an hour, but today hardly any cars are coming from Benidorm. It's eight-thirty. Very strange. He doesn't feel like going home yet, so he sits on his cooler and downs one of the cans. One turns into three. There's a lizard in front of him, so still it looks like pumice stone.

"Can I get a beer or are you going to neck the lot?"

Michela has stopped the car in front of him at the lights. She's been driving all afternoon, she got as far as Murcia working out what she was going to say to him, and then came straight back to where she knows he'll be when he's broke, which he is virtually every weekend.

"How many do you want? I haven't sold a thing. Nobody's going past."

"Of course not. It's a holiday tomorrow. Everyone's having a long weekend."

"Fuck."

"Want a lift home?"

"No."

Today Martin's got dark grey nails and Michela has no idea what it's a symbol of, whether it's punk or what; she can't decipher it and she likes that.

"Look in the back," Michela tells him.

Martin looks in the back seat. There's an electric guitar, a Fender, new, light, as if it was floating. Truth is, it isn't that new, Michela bought it third-hand on eBay, but she's never going to tell him that. She's not going to tell him who stole his old one either. All she knows is that without a guitar, Martin has nothing to do. No guitar, no dosh. No guitar, no band. No guitar, nothing.

"Nice," says Martin, getting into the car.

"This is the last thing I'm ever going to ask for."

"Right." He picks up the guitar. He's about to say thank you but bites his tongue.

"Think about it, you're going to play in front of god knows how many people, you'll do well out of it, you'll definitely be on TV. Chances like this don't come up twice."

"I know."

"You're welcome, by the way."

"Is it tuned?"

"He can't realise the lighter is missing, right? Otherwise, we're truly fucked," Michela says. "Best if you do it when you go and speak to him after you've played, when you're saying thanks for having me and all that. He'll be drunk so it'll be easy. But wait till he's by himself."

"I'll decide when to do it. What does he look like?"

"Here," says Michela, getting out her phone. "This is him."

She shows him a picture of Kaminski. He's beneath the Eiffel Tower, something from Instagram. He looks like a nice bloke, very sunburnt, a Romanian labourer with square hands and no neck.

"No one will suspect you."

Martin says nothing. He just looks at her.

"You've cut your hair," he says.

Michela touches her hair, it has just been cut: she did it herself before leaving the house this morning, in five minutes, without looking, without a mirror. She's ended up with it all over the place, like a new couple's bedroom.

Martin touches her hair.

"Come and have dinner at my place," she says.

Martin smiles. Michela starts the car and smiles as well; she's got a dimple on her left cheek that appears on the rare occasions that she does. She drives down the deserted road back to Benidorm. They drive in silence, a knowing kind of silence, until they get to her street, a street which leads to the sea but which turns its back on it, sneering; a pissed-off, downbeat street – a bit like Michela herself, which is why she chose to live there – where there's always somewhere to park. Except today. The whole street is full of cars. In fact, the whole neighbourhood, the whole of Benidorm is packed with cars belonging to people staying for the long weekend. Some are double-parked.

"All these fucking tourists," says Michela.

She goes round the block again. More cars and motorcycles and electric scooters, it's almost dark so there are people taking towels and fold-up chairs and children out of their boots. More streets, more going round the block, more cars. Sandwiches, bags of ice, tinto de verano.

"I know where we'll go," says Michela. She heads for an alleyway and goes straight to a construction site she just manages to squeeze the car into, driving over heaps of rubble and broken bricks, an enormous construction site next to an abandoned building. She parks. She turns off the engine. The sea is nowhere near but still makes its presence felt.

"Don't try it on with me," says Martin.

But she does try it on with him. They do it right there, in the driver's seat, like two teenagers, Michela's face lit up by the purple, then pink, then green lights from a fountain nearby, where a skinny white dog is splashing around like a maniac until it spots them and stays completely still, watching them whilst day breaks.

At dawn they have breakfast, just the two of them. They have two Red Bulls sitting in the car under a gigantic palm tree and watch how the sun comes up and crosses the shell of the building from façade to façade, from the bottom up. Martin starts to hum the theme tune for *The Wire*; it's what he always does after a fuck.

The fishermen at the port catch fuck all, men of every age and every nationality but only men, or at least it's very rare to ever see a woman with a rod or a net either on the rivers or on the sea or anywhere. That's just how it is. Martin had spent the best part of the morning sitting on the quay casting his rod without catching a sardine, his burnt face under the T-shirt covering his head. About one o'clock, a girl came up to him; she was bored of queuing for the boat tour to the island. She waved at him. A little girl with glasses and *Frozen* flip-flops.

"Hello."

Martin said nothing.

"Hey."

For a minute the girl watched the hypnotic, iridescent petrol stain, floating on the soupy water of the port.

"Isn't it hot in Benidorm," she said and threw a big chunk of her sandwich to the fat, black fish that looked like something out of a sci-fi film. Martin looked up.

"Don't throw them bread."

"Why not."

"Because if you feed the fish, they won't bite my hook."

"Oh, okay."

The girl curled up her toes in her flip-flops; she had pink nails. She counted to seven in English very loudly. Three times. When Martin wound in his line to change the hook, the girl threw another bit of bread, and the fish swam towards the crumbs like torpedoes.

"I told you not to throw them bread, for fuck's sake."

"Right."

She had small, narrow, gappy teeth. The next piece of bread she threw was the size of a fist. Martin looked at the child. She smiled. She screwed up her eyes, then she pulled up her shirt to show her belly and stuck out her tongue.

"You've got to be fucking kidding me." Martin leapt up, took off his right flip-flop and whacked it hard a couple of times across her hand. One and two.

The silence spoke volumes.

The girl was so surprised, she opened her mouth, but no words came out. Then she shut it again. She turned round and walked off very quickly on her flat little feet. Martin sat down again and started fishing. A few minutes later the girl, who knew her constitutional rights like all children these days, came back. She had gone straight to the Port Police to report him, the precocious little fucker. The officer on duty she came back with happened to be Michela. When Michela turned up, she stood there, looking at Martin. Her hair was tied back as tight as her uniform trousers and shirt.

"Documents."

That was the first time they ever saw each other. She stood looking at his identity card for a good couple of minutes. Then she gave it back to him and stood looking at his brown legs, the back of his neck, his big hands.

Michela threw the sandwich into the dustbin and told the girl to go back to where she'd come from.

Michela doesn't like people who call the police.

That was five years ago.

Oliver is one of those people who hangs out with people much younger than himself; he's nearly twenty but he always goes around with secondary school kids who lower their voices whenever he comes near, turn and watch him whenever he walks past, know him by name. Oliver knows. Like he knows that people his own age don't turn and watch him and that nobody ever comes looking for him. Especially the girls. He's not reached big bully status, he's not the alpha male, leader of a pack of teenagers on bikes, he's just a loner who's out of place wherever he happens to be. To Michela, Oliver seems too easy to manipulate, he's more afraid than angry, which is something she can't stand, but precisely because of that, because she can't bear him, she finds him interesting.

"What are you doing here?" Michela asks him.

They're at the entrance to the villa where the party is being held, a finca on the way to Terra Mítica with a whole palm grove, a plot so large that everyone on the east coast of Spain knows about it, a set of gates like a Californian ranch, an outside broadcast unit from local TV, swarming security detail, spotlights, helicopters, the setting sun.

"Same as you."

Michela starts laughing. She finds some of Oliver's outfits a bit of a worry, she doesn't get them, too urban, very un-Benidorm: today he's in some terrible singlet, like an Italian in a fifties film. It's the first time she's seen him like this. It looks like he's wearing a chain with a medal like some provincial grandee, but it's a tattoo of a medallion of the Jesús del Gran Poder.

"I don't believe it," she says.

"I've been invited."

"Sure. Course you have."

Oliver gets out his phone and shows her.

"Look. Here. On the list."

It's true. There's the invitation, beautifully done, with a QR code and everything so that nobody can gatecrash.

"Who invited you?"

"Anton. Somebody I know."

Michela doesn't like it one bit that Oliver could get in, bump into Martin, talk to him and scupper everything. Besides, Oliver is one of those people you never see, who's gone before saying goodbye, someone you don't miss until you realise that they've been there the whole time, listening to every word and watching every movement, without opening their mouth.

"Are you going in like that?" Michela blurts out. Oliver looks at his outfit.

"Yeah, sure. No?" He raises his eyebrows. "No?"

"Absolutely not. Go home and put something else on."

Oliver shrugs his shoulders.

"It's no big deal. No one's going to notice what I'm wearing. They're Russians."

"Suit yourself."

Oliver heads off to the entrance. Michela soon loses sight of him amongst the crowd, the flashes, the journalists, the instagrammers. She thinks on her feet. She'll take Oliver to one side to tell him they're doing a comedy and Martin to another to tell him they're doing a drama, like all good film directors, but she, Michela, will have the last laugh.

The party has already started. It's difficult to say when a party starts, ones like these tend to start when more people have arrived than there's room for, but that isn't really going to happen at this villa that's bigger than the whole of Valencia. There's a whiff of sophistication in the air, a shimmering aura, full flow, which each of the guests wears differently and that determines how close you can get to them. There are the models, the beautiful girls who have done their make-up knowing nobody will dare come within five metres of them. There are the Z-listers who go about in packs of six, like beers. There are the leaders, the bosses, short, with the faces of their bullied-at-school teenage selves, almost always sitting in a corner; everyone wants to get near them and whisper something private in their ear. And then there's everyone else, clueless and crammed in beneath the great wall of fireworks, lighting up the four AM sky, champagne tears high above, like a promise you can see straight through, the sky crossed by ancient stars and new satellites, far away, but always there, where the firmament begins. Right here and far away. After the fireworks, the sulphurous smell of hell is all that's left.

*

It's half-six in the morning. The San Sebastián posse, about seventy of them, are saying goodbye in the car park, the men with pastel jerseys round their necks, the women in chunky heels. Volvos, Mercedes, a red Tesla. At the other side of the car park are the Moroccans and, to the right, the Russians with their long-legged, inscrutable women. Each group at their own point on the compass. The party is nowhere near over, these people have days left in them, but they're off to have a shower and change before coming back later that afternoon. Michela drives the patrol car around the villa's perimeter, looking for Martin, slowly, windows down, it's already hot, it smells of burnt meat and the acid smoke of fireworks.

Martin is sitting beneath a statue, talking to a girl in a kimono and Dr Martens, she's a kid talking and smoking with the conviction that her extreme youth will last as long as her hundred tattoos. Forever. The statue is of Valery Karpin. In bronze. The girl, she's from Madrid.

"Martin," calls Michela as she walks towards him.

"You're called Martin?" the girl from Madrid asks.

"He's called whatever I say."

"And who are you? His mother?"

"His parole officer."

"Straight out of a film."

"This is my film, and you're not in it."

The girl from Madrid looks at Martin. Martin shrugs his shoulders.

"Well fuck this." The girl gets up and goes, more because she's not bothered and half-asleep than anything else; you can tell by the way she slopes off, like she's got dengue fever.

"What's happened here then?" Michela asks Martin. "Why haven't you called me all night?"

"It couldn't happen."

"Explain."

"I couldn't get anywhere near Kaminski. I don't even think he was at the party. Anyway, they made us leave our phones at the door, so we didn't record anything, and we had to go through a metal detector to get in and out."

"Right. Look at me."

Martin looks up, telltale pupils.

"Get up and go home."

"How about I try when we're out of here? When he's out and about? He must leave sometimes, mustn't he?"

"I want you to get up and go home."

"Don't push it."

"Go."

But Martin doesn't go. He can't even get up, not for the life of him. He puts his hands under his arms, closes his eyes and falls asleep right there, at Karpin's feet. Michela checks the time on her phone. She looks around, Oliver might still be there, maybe she should have thought of him in the first place. She'll have to be quick. She goes to the service entrance of the main pavilion, where the bins are. The cooks are there smoking joints, dressed in white, the Cabify drivers in black, like at Capote's ball. She calls Oliver. A tungsten arc lamp shines against the dawn sky, fresh and pink like raw flesh. Oliver doesn't answer. His phone is off.

Oliver and Michela are sitting in the San Remo at night, looking at the sea and the ten-ton seagulls and the ice in the gin and tonic that's lacquered by the blue and fuchsia neon glowing above their heads. The San Remo is Michela's favourite bar, her second office; in the San Remo, you can say what you like, and nothing happens. To be fair, in Benidorm you can do what you like, and nothing happens. Unless they call in the Spanish Legion. Which they've been known to do. She ran into Oliver a while ago, handing out flyers in the centre, filthy flyers because he kept picking them up when the tourists threw them on the ground. Leaning on a corner, in the shade, at four in the afternoon, pissed off. His fingers were yellow from the ink and had a hundred paper cuts on the tips. She whistled at him, and Oliver got in the car without a second thought. There are two types of crooks: ones who pick pockets and ones who pick people up at street corners. Michela is one of the second type too.

"So, who got you the invite to the party?" asks Michela, having a sip of her gin.

"One of Kaminski's security guys, Anton, he's a mate of his from here."

"Where do you know him from?"

"AA."

"I wouldn't have had you down as an alcoholic."

"That's why we're anonymous," laughed Oliver. "No, seriously, I don't drink, my dad did, so I never touch a drop. I go to meetings, because I'm always sober and they think I've got iron willpower, so they call me when they think they're about to fall off the wagon."

"And what's the point of all that?"

"Same as you."

"Which is?"

"Information. And trust. This Anton is always calling me, he's super shy and doesn't say very much, even though he speaks four or five languages. Maybe he's not that shy, just Russian. I don't know."

"And he knows Kaminski."

"He's his mate, as well as security."

Michela closes her eyes.

"Are you feeling alright?" Oliver asks after a while.

"Absolutely. What time is it?"

"Three."

"No one waiting at home for you?"

"No one's waiting for me anywhere."

Oliver shrugs his shoulders. He's either not bothered or doesn't get the hint. He's gobbling olives one after the other and spitting the stones as far as he can. He's got dark, brown rings under his eyes, like a sixty-year-old.

"Get a napkin," Michela says suddenly.

"What?"

"Get a napkin. And a pen. Oi, you," she says to the waiter, a blond with a buzz cut who lives at the bar, upstairs, in the storage room. "Get us a pen."

Oliver raises his eyebrows like dogs do when they're asking something. When the waiter brings the biro, Michela points Oliver to the napkin.

"Write. When's your birthday?"

"October. The third. Why?"

"Long way off." Michela gestures. "Write down everything you want for your birthday as if it was today. But not things you can buy or presents or stuff from your family. Things that you want to happen."

"Things I want to do."

"That's it."

"Are you pissed?"

"Of course. But you are too."

Oliver picks up the pen.

"Okay then, let's do this."

Oliver sits looking at the sea and sky like they were a screen with a projection for his eyes only. He tugs his upper lip and starts to write.

"You want things! Of course you do," laughs Michela after a minute.

Oliver carries on writing, line after line. The only bit of napkin he leaves free is the corner, where it says thanks for visiting.

"Right," he says, looking up.

"Let's have a look."

"What do you mean have a look?" says Oliver, covering up the napkin.

"Do you want this all to come true or not?"

"And who are you? My fairy godmother?"

"Your wicked witch. Go on, let's have a look."

They're pissed but happy pissed, low-key. It's late. Michela takes the napkin.

"You write like a seven-year-old."

She reads. There are names, places, a drawing of a house with a chimney like the houses kids draw at nursery. "CYNTHIA" written in capitals. "Learn to dance." She looks at Oliver. He's finished off all the olives.

"Now watch closely."

Slowly she folds the napkin twice lengthways then stands it on the table, on its end, like a building, her hand surprisingly steady for how drunk she is. Then she takes out a lighter and sets fire to the top edge. The paper starts to burn with a thin, blue flame and, after a few seconds, the napkin starts to lift away from the table, a couple of centimetres at first, then suddenly it shoots above their heads, crackling and sizzling.

"Voilà."

In a few seconds more, it's several metres up, floating like a ghost in flames until the fire consumes it and all that's left is a blue flash, spinning around up there, blue and yellow.

"Mind blown," whispers Oliver.

The pair of them sit there staring at the point where now there's nothing left.

"Let's go to Mítico and get something to eat," says Michela.

They go to the car, it's parked behind the skyscrapers, in the long, narrow corridor that sits between the high, treeless rocks of the mountains and the buildings, the cliff, the precipice the sun never reaches, the mountain pushing the thousand skyscrapers towards the sea, for nothing.

Benidorm Yacht Club was one of Kyle's favourite places when he lived here, ever since the summer of '76, the first time he put his British foot on Iberian soil, on the Continent. Michela knew because sometimes she'd see him from above, from the viewing platform; she'd watch him sitting there on the café terrace, where he never took her for a drink, knocking back a gin and tonic, alone and silent. Today, at this time, ten in the morning, the club's diving students are getting ready to go out on their boat, walking up and down the quayside in their wetsuits, like a sideshow in the insane headline act that is Benidorm and the whole Costa. Michela is waiting for Sorayo, a man from Seville who has been fishing at the quay ever since they put the sea there. Sorayo comes up to her, he's got skin like a leather jacket and is carrying the four fish he's caught in a plastic bag in one hand and the latest iPhone in the other. When he gets to the table, he stops and looks at Michela for a good ten seconds.

"You're getting old, Miguela," he says, getting himself a chair. He sits down.

"Why did you want to see me?"

Sorayo takes the little plate with the almonds, empties himself a handful and pockets them for later.

"To talk about your father."

"What about my father."

"He's got himself into a bit of bother. He'll never say anything so I'm here to instead."

"You don't know anything about my father."

"Right. Neither do you."

Sorayo's nails are black with tar but he's got that healthy, beautiful glow people have when they spend a lot of time by the sea.

"So, what's the story?"

"A Russian. A Russian and your father Kyle, right here yesterday," he says, pointing to the table where they were sitting. "They started having a row. They weren't talking very loudly but they were definitely having a row, and they definitely meant it."

"What about? Who was the Russian?"

"No idea. I don't know."

"What were they speaking?"

"English."

"You speak English?"

"I don't speak-speak, but I understand everything. You don't think I come to the club just for that, do you?" he said, pointing to the bag with the fish.

"They weren't talking about a cigarette lighter, were they?"

Sorayo shrugged his shoulders.

"Could have been. The Russian had red hair, wispy little beard, rough skin. Know what I mean."

"And what was the Russian saying?"

"The Russian. No, I don't know. You couldn't move for all the tourists, and I couldn't always hear them properly. And all those paellas."

"What time yesterday?"

"I don't know what happened or what your father said to the Russian, or maybe it was the other way round and he said something to your father, but suddenly the Russian started shouting and then they were full-on scrapping right there" – he points to the kerb – "right there on the ground."

Michela looks at the kerb. There's a dark stain, could be fish guts, cooking oil, motor oil. She doesn't like the look of it at all.

"Your father's face looked alright. I think his body took the brunt of it."

"Do you know where he is?"

"No. I only know what people are up to when they're here. As soon as I can't see them, they don't exist. Like on telly. That's just how it is."

"A Russian."

"You've got to find Kyle. Even if he doesn't want to be found: I know all about that... He's too past it to be getting involved in this sort of bother. If you're old, Miguela, imagine what he is now."

When Sorayo clears off, Michela stays put in the club. She lights a cigarette and immediately throws it away. She orders a vermouth. She downs it and asks for another vermouth. She listens to the wind in the flags and the sails, impatient, insistent, flapping the towels on the sand, off in the distance. There's an empty table in front of her with a Cinzano ashtray and a Spanish toothpick holder. Many summers ago, she once sat at that table with Kyle. It might not have been that one exactly, but she can definitely remember it was the last one on the terrace, it was night-time, and, as always, it was summer. Kyle was smoking. It had turned chilly so he was wearing a raincoat like a French detective from a film over his swimming trunks, and he was smoking. Camels. The box was there on the table and next to the box, Reggie Kray's lighter, which Kyle hardly ever took out because he was worried about losing it. Michela's eyes were fixed on the lighter, she must have been about eight years old, maybe ten, she was drinking Fanta, not even Coca-Cola, so she must have been more or less that old. Kyle was knocking back a gin and tonic. Suddenly he looked at her as if he was snapping back to this century, to this country, to Benidorm of all places. He smiled. Then he pointed at the napkin dispenser and told her to get a napkin. Michela took one and held it up. Kyle asked the waiter for a biro and gave it to Michela. Then he said, "Write down the things you'd like to happen to you, five of them," and stretched out the long, knotty fingers of his right hand whilst he carried on smoking. "Anything?" Kyle nodded. Michela picked up the pen, she was left-handed, she is left-handed, and her handwriting was poor like a semi-literate, she wrote in capitals and in red because it was a red pen. She only wrote down three things. Not five. As if at that age she already knew something that nobody aged eight is meant to know. When she'd finished, she passed the napkin to Kyle. Kyle took it. "Now watch." Then he folded the napkin lengthways and stood it up on the table. He lit the lighter. He winked at her. Did he wink at her? That might have happened after the event in her imagination, subsequently, not on that September night in real life. He lit the lighter and set fire to the top edge of the napkin. The napkin rose off the table, first for a few seconds to the level of Michela's eyes, where to her astonishment it started to burn properly, then suddenly, it flew up. One metre, three, and there, like the special effects in a cheap film, it vanished into the air, with the sizzle and splutter of an Elizabethan witch. Kyle stared at the sky. Smiling. Nothing else. Michela looked down on the table where the flakes of ash had gently started to fall, black ash rain, settling in scarce little piles. The leftovers of a cremation. Then she looked at Kyle. He was reading a book. Michela wondered what all this had been in aid of, why he hadn't read her list of wishes. Or probably, even by that point, she wondered nothing at all. This was just how it was.

She's called all the clinics and hospitals in Benidorm, asking whether her father, Kyle McKay, has been admitted, but all of them tell her they've had nobody of that name until the Marina Baixa confirms that an Englishman of Kyle's age was admitted the day before unconscious and without documents. So Michela sets off for the hospital. She doesn't like hospitals, mostly because she can't bear nurses, or anybody else, telling her what she can and can't do or where she can and can't go. The corridor is very long, mint green, it seems much longer to Michela than it actually is. At the end, there are a couple of IV stands, some kid looking at their phone, a fifty-year-old bloke in a polo shirt having a go at a nurse three times his size. When she opens the door, she sees straight away that the Englishman isn't her father. Michela recognises him; he's one of the old regulars at the police station, a Man U fan who's lived in Benidorm for forty years and doesn't speak a single word of Spanish. The room has no windows. There's a poster of Benidorm instead, to perk it up a bit. A poster of the buildings, not the sea. The glare of the neon light is very white, like an empty fridge, the Englishman's skin is like opal, like somebody who only goes out at night and never sees sunlight. He's sitting on the bed, wide awake.

When Michela has made sure it's not Kyle, she heads for the door to leave.

"I know you," says the Englishman.

"I know you too."

"You've always got a face on even though you're lovely-looking."

"Whatever you say."

"Will you pay for my telly? It's three euros a day."

"Look after yourself," says Michela, opening the door.

"You too. You're going to need it. Remember me to your father."

Michela stops.

"You know Kyle?"

"Everybody knows Kyle."

"Where is he?"

The old man smiles, and it takes twenty years off him in a stroke.

"I'll tell you if you pay for my telly. No one comes to see me, but the ones who do come are mean sods."

"Alright," Michela agrees. She waits. The Englishman raises his bushy white eyebrows.

"Well?"

"Right this minute?"

"It's five o'clock."

Michela goes out of the room, goes to the reception desk, pays the three euros rental. When she gets back, she finds the Englishman watching some reality show about glass-blowers.

"I can't remember," says the Englishman. "We saw each other on Tuesday, it must have been Tuesday, I think, at the Basques and we were talking for a while, you know what your father's like, he only talks when he's got a drink in him."

Michela hasn't a clue when her father talks or doesn't.

"You don't remember anything else? Is he alright? Was there anybody else with you?"

"I don't even remember where I've been this morning."

"I can see."

"We were watching them play pelota, I do remember that. In Poniente, where the zip line is."

"Know where he lives?"

"About your mother. He lives next door to some Spanish woman in the centre, there are dogs. That's it. Two at any rate."

"What about my mother?"

"He was talking about Laurana, about your mother, about her looks. About how she was a Spanish beauty. Like you."

Michela gets up to leave. He's a drunk. And that's fine.

"What are you doing here?" asks Michela from the door. "Why aren't you at home? Why haven't you got your documents with you?"

The Englishman is fiddling with the remote control, paying no attention to her.

"Because I've got no money to pay the rent, so it was either this or the nick. And I'm too old for all that now."

Sometimes people who don't want any trouble are the ones that go and fuck up your life. They elegantly extract themselves from the middle of things without you even noticing, as if they'd not been there the whole time, and, in actual fact, they hadn't. Laurana's note was very easy to read but very hard to understand. "I'm off on a trip." That's all it said, no where, no why, no for how long. The note was on top of the pillow on top of the unmade bed. Unmade for days. There was a poster of Cyndi Lauper on the wall, and on the fuchsia bedside table, covered in cigarette burns, there was a bottle of Arpège by Lanvin and a pile of *MAD* magazines and a Walkman and all the meaningless paraphernalia that in her platinum blond head represented everything that wasn't Benidorm, that represented getting away, getting away for good, getting far away to anywhere not remotely like this city. Foreign, different, exciting, and new. Modern. That's what she'd wanted to find in Kyle: a mod from *Quadrophenia*, which had just been released, someone very different from the rest of the cheap tourists in the nightclub where she sang every night till three in the morning, barefoot, huge backcombed beehive, John Player Special in her hand. The months that followed raced by in a state of bliss, a long-awaited promise suddenly fulfilled, until she realised, too late, that Kyle was a professor of modern history at Queen Mary University of London, nothing more, and much more refined than she expected, polished manners and eccentric tastes, like all Brits, someone she had nothing in common with. A gentleman. A gentleman who had come to Benidorm to write a book about English gangsters and who, more to the point, hadn't the slightest intention of going back to London. An English gentleman.

Kyle was sitting on the bed. He'd already read the note several times, each time as if it was written in a different language. He looked around to try and work out what she'd taken with her, to get an idea of how long she might be gone for. Some of Laurana's clothes were still on the floor, as if she'd decided what to take and what to leave at the last minute: those ripped jeans, this swimsuit that didn't fit, that two-year-old daughter, crawling around on the double bed, watching *La Bola de Cristal* on one of the few black-and-white TVs left in Benidorm. She'd taken her winter clothes, her proper winter clothes, an orange parka, and the black dress. The black dress in acrylic faux silk, full-length, with a neckline down to the belly button and gold chain straps; Laurana had pointed it out in a shop window in the centre of town days earlier. The following day, Kyle went back to the shop. He wanted to give her a surprise and get it for her as a present, then go out to the Ku to celebrate, despite knowing by that stage that there wasn't much to celebrate. He went into the shop, it was big and ugly, spacious. It seemed to go on for miles with ceiling lights and dozens of jackets, chinchilla and mink coats, furs that are a Benidorm classic, something Kyle never understood. He went over to look at the party dresses, badly cut, a whiff of the second-hand about them. The black dress wasn't there, nor was it in the window, he'd looked when he came in. The changing rooms were to the right. There was a bloke sitting in front of one that had its curtain drawn, English, about sixty, wiry hair, cavalry officer hair, big-boned like a farmer or someone with a title. They looked at each other for a moment. The Englishman was wearing Church's, impeccable but from fifteen years ago. Salomé's latest hit was playing in the shop. The Englishman smiled at Kyle and tapped his index finger along to the beat of Salomé's song on his crossed knee. He had a signet ring on his little finger. The changing room curtain opened, and Laurana stepped out. Wearing the black dress, arms spread, hair pulled back in a rather girlish ponytail. She took another step forward and stood in front of the Englishman. She gave him a twirl, slowly, so he could see properly, front and back. Then she bent over and gave him a peck on the cheek. The Englishman blushed. She burst out laughing, came out with something in Valencian, went back into the changing room, and shut the curtain. She hadn't seen Kyle. Kyle stood there and looked at the Englishman, his glasses misty with rage, the colour of a radish. Kyle said nothing. He said nothing in the shop, he said nothing later at home, he said nothing ever. The black dress showed the outline of her knickers.

So, off she'd gone with the black dress, and a baseball cap that brought her good luck, and her triumphant, badly timed smile. Michela had peed on the red rug beside the bed. Kyle looked at her crawling. Drool, snot. She grabbed his finger. He lifted her up off the floor and sat her down by his side on the indigo sheets. Outside, behind both their backs, the Spantax plane taking Laurana away forever was flying past, over the sharp, definitive line of the Mediterranean horizon.

"Shit moves, mate," shouts Michela above the music. "You look like you've got seven left feet."

They're at the San Remo, drinking, celebrating the fact that it's Sunday or something.

"Let's have a look at you, then," replies Oliver. "This bitch thinks she's going to tear up the dance floor."

"My arse is on fire when I dance," says Michela, getting to her feet.

They're playing Rod Stewart, "Da Ya Think I'm Sexy?". Michela loves Rod Stewart. He must have gone to the same hairdresser as Tina Turner, that mane of angry chicken feathers, which Michela tried to copy with no success when she was twenty. Michela's in boys' swimming trunks, knee-length, with a banana pattern. The manager of the San Remo lent them to her because a while ago some girl on a hen do, wearing a tiara with cocks on it, threw up on her. She's got an SD Eibar football shirt on top. She's very tanned, barefoot, and can really move.

"Watch," she tells Oliver. "Get over here and get your arms in the air."

The manager of the San Remo turns up the volume on the radio.

"Like this?"

"That's it!"

"Look. I'm twerking."

"Show me."

Oliver wiggles around: if he had any flesh on his bones, it might be alright, but the manager bursts out laughing.

"Move your head!" says Michela and smiles at him. She points to his feet then points to her own.

"Look at that pout!" says Oliver. Michela pinches his nose. "I can pout too!"

"Come on Oliver! Bring it!" Michela shakes her shoulders, claps her hands, spins round, and again.

"You two are full of crap," says the manager.

They're dancing, badly, but nobody dances badly if they get stuck in; that's what Michela tells Oliver over the music that's playing way above the decibel level that's allowed at this time of night, but nobody gives a shit. This is Benidorm. The three or four couples still around on the promenade come and join in. Oliver tries to climb up on the bar but falls off his stool. Michela is taller. She jumps. She climbs up and pulls him with her. On top of the bar, Oliver looks like Christopher Walken dancing: now he's laughing so much, Michela can see that he has a man-child face, just like Walken, and it changes so much when he smiles that he looks like a completely different person.

"D'you know the only thing missing now, Oliver?"

"A microphone."

"A haircut. Oi, turn the music down and get me a pair of scissors."

The man from the bar gets a pair of scissors, ones you cut ham with. Michela gets off the bar as best she can and sits Oliver down on a stool. Oliver shuts his eyes and Michela starts to cut his hair, a few random snips of his thin hair, falling to the floor like raining ash. It's Billy Joel's turn to sing, the waiters and the customers have nothing better to do than watch Michela cut Oliver's hair. Despite the fact that it's three in the morning and she's totally off her face, and the scissors are shit, she gives him a very professional-looking mullet. When she's finished, Oliver looks in the tinted mirror on the wall. When he smiles, he has a dimple in his left cheek.

Benidorm Island, a rock with a Spanish flag on top, sinking irreversibly into a five-metre abyss, covered with thorny bushes and seagull feathers and guano. It's Michela's favourite place when she's sick of everyone, which is basically every evening, every day of the week. It's gone nine. She's meeting Oliver at nine-thirty. She's sitting on a smooth rock that's burning her arse. She trains her binoculars on Playa Poniente, hoping to see him appear at any minute. The last tourists from the island tour are already leaving, Michela watches how the tour boat slowly casts off and heads towards Mal Pas beach, towards the coast where at this time of day the mountains are the same colour and texture as the cork bags on sale in the centre of town. Oliver suddenly appears in the binoculars' double field of vision in his motorboat, a mini 007. Michela waves at him and climbs down, rock by rock, until she gets to the island's jetty. She jumps onto her boat and starts the motor; she has no idea how to drive it, it's big and old and confiscated from some Moroccans who were using it to ferry illegal immigrants; as camouflage, it's painted the same colour as the sea at sunset. Michela goes round the island, then about five hundred metres further out to sea, steering a little towards Finestrat. She stops the engine. She sees Oliver arriving in his boat.

"Here?" Oliver asks.

"Yes. This is far enough out. There'll be no Guardia Civil or coastguards or cargo ships out here."

Michela drops the anchor on her boat. She looks at the spot's coordinates on her phone and memorises them. She puts the phone away. Then she jumps onto Oliver's boat and points the prow in the direction of Playa Poniente, where the sun is melting, sinking, disappearing.

The skyscrapers are starting to light up like equalisers on a mixing deck. Everything comes with music, in Benidorm.

Too many tattoos for so little to say. Too many tattoos, Calvin Klein labels, number one cuts; his body has more clues than a Sunday crossword. Although he wants to come across as modern, Anton is an old-school Russian, real, hardcore, all white nights on the banks of the Volga, eating raw meat and knocking back the vodka.

"What's this Anton like, then?" Michela asked Oliver. Oliver had bought himself clothes, a beanie pulled down to his ears, new watch, as if he was launching a new life that warranted it all. They were sitting by the window of a bar in a petrol station near Terra Mítica, the sun was setting and the reflections from truck windscreens kept crossing from one end of the bar to the other like a ping-pong rally.
 "He's sad."

Anton and Oliver don't have much in common, only the very Chekhovian, very Mediterranean habit of sitting on a step eating sunflower seeds, talking till all hours. Now they're walking up one of the streets that goes to the bus station, an uphill slope that gives a hint of the mountains nearby. Anton called Oliver half an hour ago because he'd had the sudden urge to chuck a vermouth into his body, his nearly six-foot-four body, with its small, round, low-set ears like an ex-con. A vermouth with a slice of fresh cucumber, he'd said. He's swaying a bit as he walks, as if he's already drunk, but that's just his nerves. Oliver is leading the way. Anton is walking with his hands behind his back, like a minister. It's midday.

"Does he drive? Does he have a car?" Michela asked. Outside on the forecourt, the petrol pumps looked like they were surrounded by halos of heat, like acid trips.

"An electric one."

"Could you get hold of it?"

Oliver chewed a soggy chip. He thought about it.

"Yeah. But I can't drive."

"That rules that out, then."

Oliver stops for a minute at El Rápido, a tiny café with a hatch out on the street. He asks for two coffees to take away. Whilst they're making them, he looks at Anton's reflection in the café window. When Anton realises, he looks away.

"This street is dead," says Anton. He pronounces dead like a Spaniard.

"It's Sunday," says Oliver.

They carry on up the hill; it keeps getting steeper. And quieter. Anton puts some nicotine gum in his mouth.

"And the house," asked Michela, and ordered another beer from the waiter, pointing to one of the four cans that were on the table. "What's it like?"

"I don't get it." Oliver thought about it for a minute. He said it with conviction, like somebody who's used to making decisions. "The house is full of people all the time, I've no idea if they're Kaminski's relatives or what, but like twenty people live there, girlfriends, nieces, nephews, all that. There are loads of rooms, some with nothing in them, no furniture, just people. It's big, lots of staircases and patios. It's like the Casino Mediterráneo, easy to get in, very difficult to leave."

Oliver turns left. They walk into a squalid little street, tarmac bubbling from the heat and tall, yellow weeds at the bottom edges of the two-storey buildings. There's a smell of warm rubbish; the dustbin lorries don't make it to this neighbourhood. Anton follows him.

"Has he got a girlfriend?"

Michela suddenly got up. She picked up her belt, where she kept the tools of her trade: pistol, truncheon, radio. She got up because she'd had an idea, something had come to her when she saw the big oil stain in the middle of the forecourt where two lorry drivers were starting a bare-knuckle punch-up.

"In Rostov, he's got a girlfriend who sends him dirty vids every so often. Not as often as he'd like."

"So, nobody here, then."

Oliver shook his head. He adjusted his green beanie and looked at his reflection in the window.

"He says sadness is all the stuff that never happens."

"Cute."

*

Oliver is silent as he walks. He crumples the paper cup and throws it on the ground. Then he stops and bends over to tie up a shoelace, despite not having shoelaces. Oldest trick in the book. He fixes his eyes on Anton's back, whom he's been following and who is now a few metres ahead, hands deep in his pockets, looking at the ground, talking to himself in Russian.

"Anton!" Oliver shouts.

When he hears, Anton stops in his tracks and turns round to look at Oliver. At that very moment, on that very spot, someone throws a whole bucket of dirty water out of a window, and it lands on Anton.

"Bollocks."

Soaked from head to toe.

"Fuck!"

Anton shouts something out in Russian. It doesn't sound good.

"For fuck's sake!" says Oliver.

Anton still has his eyes shut; he's dripping with the filthy water. He roars like a bear. Oliver comes up to him.

"Are you okay?"

Anton spits out some water and wipes his face with his hand.

"Shit. What a fucking mess."

Anton looks down at his body, his clothes, the ground, everything. He says something in Russian that sounds like grinding sand.

"It came from the second floor. I saw," says Oliver.

"Are you sure?"

"Yeah. Look," Oliver says, pointing up. "From that window."

Anton looks up; in the open window, there's a flowerpot with nothing in it. He shouts. Nobody appears. He shouts something in Russian and goes to the entrance, which is half open, the door jammed with a wedge.

He climbs the stairs three at a time. He gets to the front door of the flat, wooden, black varnish, and a Christ with his hand up as if he's directing traffic above the peephole. He bashes on the door a couple of times with flat of his hand.

The door opens.

Today Michela has got the Taser, it's the first time she's used it, her debut, she's smiling from ear to ear, her dimple's there and everything.

The Taser works like a charm.

The weight and proportional spread of the other empire in Benidorm, Russian rather than British, is approximately twenty stone of Slavic matter, distributed over a six-foot-four-inch body, belonging, in this case, to Anton Markovich, ex-third-division footballer, ex-bodyguard, ex-anonymous alcoholic. Oliver has found out around the place that Anton is the grandson of Igor Markovich, the first Russian in the tourist vanguard that invaded in the seventies. He came up with the very brilliant, very Crimean seaside resort idea of renting out deckchairs on the beach, which he turned into a business that has had three generations of Markoviches rubbing their hands with glee and speaking impeccable Spanish, with a hint of Russian rhetoric, with a hint of a Valencian accent. Getting Anton's body down the stairs, carrying it into Michela's car, and from Michela's car onto the beach has already taken them a good couple of hours. Michela and Oliver have managed to get him out of the car between them, and holding him under his armpits they've dragged him in the forty-degree heat like your average Tuesday morning drunk, through the crowd of unaccompanied children and alabaster French tourists and women in hijabs, right to the far end of the beach where Michela has tied up her Zodiac. His toecaps scraped and squeaked the whole way along the Playa Poniente promenade.

"Do you think he'll wake up?" asks Oliver.

"Yes. In three months. I've given him a couple of pills."

They dump him, motionless, on the bottom of the boat. He's in Michela's sunglasses and a pair of black studded cowboy boots that look awful with his pink Fred Perry T-shirt.

"Can I keep the boots?" says Oliver, looking down at his own sellotaped-together Nikes.

"When we're done with all this," says Michela, starting the engine. They pull off a few metres, towards some hot Italian men swimming about together, and a herd of seven kids clinging on to the same inflatable, who scream in unison when the Zodiac almost passes on top of them.

Michela accelerates, Oliver grabs on to his seat as hard as he can. In twenty minutes, they arrive at the boat they've anchored out at sea, in the middle of nowhere, an abandoned Pontiac in the middle of the burnt Nevada desert. Anton slips as they try to get him out of the Zodiac and falls into the water, he goes under for a few seconds, then reappears floating face up like a little Orthodox miracle, or as if he was full of laughing gas. Between the two of them, they get him onto the boat. Like a scene from one of Berlanga's films. Fuck the Russian. They take a good, long look at him, flat out, face up on the deck, his eyes half open, drugged. He's got such a fat tongue. Afterwards they drag him into the cabin, he's still completely out for the count, and he'll probably stay that way till the following day, when he'll wake up, not remember a thing, and not have a clue where he is. He looks like a romantic alcoholic, one of those romantics who drinks to stop being romantic, but ends up being more so. Oliver takes off the cowboy boots, one after the other. A lot of boot for such tiny, delicate, smooth feet. He puts the boots on. They look fantastic on him.

"Ready," he says.

They jump into the Zodiac and set off.

They leave two kilos of cooked ham on the boat; there are four loaves of bread, a dozen oranges, and ten litres of water. There's no motor, no rudder, and no way of knowing which way the coast is.

Today has been a useful day, exemplary in its own way, straight to the point, no messing about. Michela holds off making any kind of judgement about it, waiting for a better occasion.

Back on dry land, they pick up the car and take the long, twisty, tree-lined road up to the Benidorm Cross. Michela picks up Anton's phone, which she turned off when she took it from him hours ago. When she turns it back on, there are fifteen calls and more than forty messages. They are in the car, they've parked at the entrance to the esplanade, the wind is so strong out here that it feels like it might blow down the stone cross and the whole of Christianity with it, but even so there's the odd gang of teenagers getting plastered under the accusatory glare of the spotlights and a couple of tourists admiring the flora: thyme, scrub, and used condoms. It's ten at night. Michela puts the radio on.

She doesn't like silence. It's for old people.

Oliver is sprawled out on the back seat, with his feet up against the open window, admiring his new cowboy boots. He is drinking a Monster as if nothing's up, as if a kidnapping was entirely run of the mill for a Tuesday afternoon.

"How much are you going to ask for?" he asks Michela. Then yawns. He's that age.

"Seventy grand."

"Seventy grand! Fuck off."

"How much would you ask for?"

"Kaminski's stinking rich."

"It's not about how much Kaminski's got but how much Anton's worth."

"He's his friend."

"There are lots of different types of friends."

"He's his friend."

"How much would you pay for your best friend?"

Oliver shuts up at that. He doesn't have any best friends. He has people he knows, no-hopers he's mixed up in scams with, colleagues, people he wouldn't risk a penny or a moment of his life for, and what's worse, people who wouldn't give a penny for him either.

"I'm going for a smoke," he says, opening the door with his foot, out of sorts.

He goes out and stands in the wind. Michela stares at him. There are many types of thieves, but she divides them into two groups: thieves you can spot a mile off, and those you can't. Yobs, hustlers, chavvy girls, and wide boys who take selfies for Instagram with the ride they've just swiped, and the devious shits with side partings who look like butter wouldn't melt. Michela only trusts the first sort, which is why she trusts Oliver, who's lit his fag and is smoking looking out to the sea down below. Michela takes Anton's phone. She looks at the photos, he's got loads, Anton eating in Japanese restaurants, Anton with four friends in suit and tie imitating the *Reservoir Dogs* poster, Anton sunbathing in Florida. She finds a picture of the girl from Madrid at the party, with Kaminski, the two of them hugging in the snow at night, she's in a bikini and Ugg boots. So, there's something going on between the girl from Madrid and Kaminski. He looks happy to be with her and she looks happy to be in the photo. She can't waste time looking at more selfies. She can't risk them locating the phone. She looks for the last chat between Anton and Kaminski. She sends Kaminski a photo they took in the flat of Anton tied to the radiator with duct tape, drugged and out of it.

She writes:

TOMORROW CASA DE FREDDY OO.OO.
ANTON FOR KRAY'S LIGHTER.

Then she writes the address for Casa de Freddy. Kaminski is online.

Michela sends the message. Double blue tick.

Kaminski is still online.

Oliver smokes slowly, the wind blowing his T-shirt, his over-baggy jeans hanging around his legs like an old junkie; the only things that seem to anchor him to the ground are the stolen boots, heavy and solid, firm roots against the storm.

Kaminski is still online. He doesn't reply.

Oliver comes back to the car and smiles at Michela.

Kaminski has gone offline. He hasn't replied. He hasn't called. What does that mean. If he has to think about it, it's not a good sign, if he's waiting so he can track the phone, it's not a good sign, if he doesn't give a shit about Anton, it couldn't be a worse sign. In any case, she has to dump the phone as soon as possible. Michela turns it off, gets out of the car and goes over to Oliver. She looks at the phone one last time.

"Everything okay?"

"More or less," Michela replies.

She hurls the phone down the mountain. In mid-fall, it hits a rock, and its torch comes on, and as it continues its nosedive, it traces a thousand somersaults in the air, zig-zagging, hurtling into rocks like a demented asteroid, like Kennedy's bullet, until it hits an outcrop and shoots off in an endless, perfect parabola that finishes up in the sea.

"And what do I get out of all this?" Oliver asks.

They're sitting in Michela's Zodiac about two hundred metres from the boat anchored out at sea. Michela is looking at Anton through her binoculars, checking on his movements, making sure he's still there. Anton can't see them. It's almost night. Anton is bored and more than likely seasick.

"My protection."

"Protection from what. If I don't do anything."

"This has to be more fun than anything you've ever done before in your life."

"Yes. Definitely."

Oliver is quiet for a minute.

"But there's much more fun I could have."

It was that five-second pause that got Michela's guard up. There wasn't a shred of doubt in Oliver's voice, and if he felt no fear or doubt, then something wasn't quite right.

"We'll talk about it," she said to him.

"When."

"Shut it, Gobby."

Oliver is suddenly quiet. He goes pale. Gobby, The Gob, that's what they called him at school because he never stopped talking.

Michela passes Oliver the binoculars.

"Look," she says. "Have a good look what he's got in his hand. I can't make it out."

Oliver takes the binoculars and focuses them on the boat. Michela looks at Oliver carefully. Weighing him up.

"I can't see anything weird," he says, getting up.

He's so small. Tiny. Scrawny. How old is Oliver? Who does he live with?

"I think he's asleep."

What does he do with his life? Who does he talk to about stuff? Who would miss him? Michela looks around slowly. They're out at sea. Nobody would see or hear anything. Total silence. Oliver lowers the binoculars, shrugs his shoulders. When he goes to sit down, he looks at the seat and stops.

"Put that away," he tells Michela.

"Why? Don't you like it?"

"No."

"You can touch it if you like."

"No."

"Touch it."

A seagull flies past, looking at them.

"I said no."

"Fine. No problem," says Michela, picking up the pistol from the seat. She puts it away. "I don't need to show it to know that I've got it."

La Casa de Freddy was one of the first Benidorm megaclubs, halfway up the steep road to the Sierra Gelada, right on the edge of the mountain ridge. Now it's just ruins, where kids come first for frights, then for fumbles, the haunted house for the whole town, the set for free-to-view pornos and a hideout for junkies and Moroccans just off the traffickers' small boats. Michela has come alone, walking for nearly an hour, so she doesn't have to leave her car where somebody might see it. When she got there, she checked that the coast was clear and hid behind some thorny bushes about a hundred metres above the old disco. It's ten-thirty. There's an hour and a half before midnight, the time she told Kaminski to meet her. She wants to know what she's dealing with, if he understood the message, or not, or what. There's nothing moving in the ruins of the club, the road is deserted, and there's no noise except the endless soundtrack of the wind, blustering in all directions. A wind with a voice of its own, serious, reverberating. A hurricane roaring more and more powerfully, more and more furiously through the branches of the trees, looking for a fight, until suddenly, off in the distance, the crack of a tree starting to break, to tear apart with the force of the wind. The scream from a falling tree is long and deep, it demands respect as the tree splinters and shatters until it breaks completely and collapses on the undergrowth, exhaling like a choir in full voice. Kaminski doesn't show. A couple of Romanians who must live in the disco have emerged and are now making their way down the road with their hands deep in their pockets to make sure the wind doesn't blow them away. Michela looks at her phone. It's gone twelve. Someone lights a bonfire in the building, in a corner against a wall, although there's no sign of anyone, as if the fire has been lit by spontaneous combustion. The building has a life of its own, ghosts of the disco. Still no sign of life from Kaminski. Every so often, Michela takes out her night-vision binoculars, looks at the empty building, the bonfire, the glowing white eyes of the creatures and the rats and the lizards who live in the weeds. Kaminski doesn't show up. The wind has died down, has become gentler, hardly makes a sound. It's twelve-thirty. She's so far up the mountain that she can see the gleaming eyes of the seagulls, gliding through the air in front of her, hanging there, hardly moving, looking at her. For a minute, she thinks about Kyle, where he might be at that moment, how he is, whether there's such a thing as criminal poetry, and what she should ask him when she sees him.

Suddenly, the embers of a cigarette light up at the far end of the club. She sees it through a hole in the roof, which a hundred Mediterranean hurricanes have shattered. The embers light up a man's face. Two men. Three. Now she can hear their voices. They're speaking Russian. Almost immediately, she sees the three leaving the club, none of them are Kaminski, three big bastards, Michela wouldn't even reach their waists, where they keep their 9 mm Berdyshes. They got tired of waiting for her, they must have been here for hours, sitting in the dark, not saying a word. She just got away without them seeing her. Now the three of them are walking down the road together, one is on his phone, another is in swimming trunks, as if he'd planned to go down to the beach just after pulling the trigger on whoever it was that he was there to meet that night, on Michela.

She watches them go off.

At one-thirty, she smokes a cigarette, gets up, and goes.

She goes back to the house, the one with the ficus, the so-called family home. Some days she prefers not to go to her flat, just in case, just to be on the safe side. She doesn't sleep in her teenage bedroom, but when she gets there, she goes in and sees that everything is still there, her clothes are still there, messy in the drawers, like the jumble in a teenager's head, spun out, unfocused, dirty. She puts on a Prince T-shirt and some red-and-black-striped ankle socks, because the floor is cold, the house is cold. In the sitting room, in the dark, she sits down on the wide five-seat sofa: why a five-seater, Michela never knew. Nobody ever came to the house. She leaves her service pistol on the table. She doesn't sleep. But memories come back to her like badly formed dreams. In one of these memories that keep fucking up her night, the four-thirty one, she sees Kyle at the door of the house at the same time of night, four-thirty, but years ago. Thirty years ago, or something like that. Kyle is looking for the keys so he can get out of the house because he's run out of booze, he's even finished off the Pedro Ximénez, which means serious boozing, and now he's at the door. In the dark. Looking for the keys so he can go to the Mars. But the keys aren't there. Michela has made sure they're well hidden so he can't get out. She's tucked them under the cushions on the sofa, where she's pretending to be asleep, but through her almost closed eyelids she's watching her father. She sees him searching in his raincoat pockets, on the side table by the front door, he's drunk but he's so furious about not being able to find his keys that his pulse is steady and his attention focused. He looks at Michela again. She doesn't move a muscle, like a deer dazzled by headlights. Then he lumbers over to the big window. He opens it, it creaks. Old wood. He gets one leg out, clumsily, then the other. He jumps. Outside he rubs his hands on his linen trousers. Kyle never wore jeans. Michela sees his silhouette framed by the window, a centaur in the desert. Kyle puts his hands in his pockets, filled with old-time peseta coins, small change, and goes out through the gate. He leaves it open. Michela sits up on the sofa, like she is doing right now, arms crossed, leaning slightly forward, like when you want to get up and leave.

"Who's there," she suddenly says out loud. But there's nobody there and she knows it.

The next morning, she picks up a rubbish bag and puts all her stuff in it. She locks the door with the same keys she used to hide every night, and throws the rubbish bag in the bin. She won't come back again.

"Kyle's not in," says the woman, Spanish, white hair, glasses like jam jars, through the half-open door of the flat opposite.

Michela has been knocking at the door to her father's flat for a while. El Potro has given her Kyle's address, a flat in a beehive of a building, with a huge twenty-four-hour tobacconist crammed with tourists buying duty-free boxes of fags, all day, all night. El Potro and Kyle met a couple of days ago and ended up there sleeping off their hangovers after a night at the Roxy on Calle Génova. I told him to ring you, El Potro told Michela after giving her the address. But he hasn't.

"Do you know when he'll be back?"

The woman shakes her head. She's barefoot and her toe-nails are painted black. There's barking coming from Kyle's flat, and scratches at the door.

"Has he got dogs?"

"Two" – the woman puts up two fingers – "Gizmo and Fernando."

"Is Kyle alright?"

"Same as always." As Michela is in uniform, the woman looks like she's not sure what's going on. "Who are you?"

Michela goes back and raps on the door with her knuckles.

"I've told you he's not there," says the woman again.

"I'm his daughter."

The woman furrows her brow.

"Kyle's not got kids."

Then she shuts the door.

"Do not sit down," says Rob. Today there are ten, twelve Grants, they're in a cellar taking the plastic covers off five new billiard tables that have just arrived. Rob has a white ball in one hand and a red one in the other. "Who said you could sit down."

Michela is still on her feet. She's not shown the slightest intention of sitting down, but she says nothing. The plastic wrappings are piling up behind her on the billiard tables, they look like glaciers. The image is too weird.

"You've got yourself into something way out of your league, Mike."

"And somehow I've got to get myself out of it."

"The Kaminskis. You've got to be bastard kidding," says Rob. Then he smashes the two balls together; the noise leaves nothing to the imagination.

Michela doesn't know where she stands now when it comes to Kaminski. She's come here pretty sure that the Grants would protect her, like they always do, but it's one thing to be protected in the Spanish National Police Force, Benidorm Division, where nobody has laid a finger on her for fifteen years, and another when she's mixed up with the Kaminskis and hundreds of millions of Russians. She hasn't a clue how many there are; a lot, she imagines. But she's come with an ace up her sleeve, which she plays now, face up on the green baize of the billiard table.

Michela and the Grants' last little escapade together had been with a man from Madrid with a house in Altea. He'd started a petition for an eco-tax on tourists who wanted access to the beaches the whole way along the coast. The English, from Leeds or Liverpool or wherever, didn't see the funny side, but it turned out the man from Madrid was getting far more signatures than anyone was expecting. The Grants didn't want to have to break his legs, or make him a martyr to his cause and have hundreds and hundreds more idiots from Madrid following in his footsteps, so they left it up to Michela. She played it cool, simply planted a hundred pots of marijuana on the patio of his house in Altea and raided him the following day. It was in all the papers. Now the man from Madrid is set to disappear for a good stretch, if he comes back at all. Rob wanted to give Michela a Honda to say thanks, but she turned it down. She preferred to bank the favour till it suited her to call it in. Today, she's calling it in.

"I did warn you."

"Don't count on me for anything else."

As soon as she says it, she bites her tongue. Rob, who has been bashing the balls together all this time, suddenly stops. The nine Grants in the background are shit-faced, one of them lies down on the billiard table to sleep it off and a few seconds later all four legs break underneath him. The rest of them burst out laughing, gold-toothed laughing. All except Rob.

"Look," he says to Michela, "you've got me on a good day. Otherwise, see this?"

He points to a billiard cue.

"You know where I'd be shoving it."

"Forget what I said. It just came out."

Rob puts the balls down on the table, slowly, and crosses his arms, it's not a massive deal, they can both see that.

"Venga," says Rob, "let's get some air."

Six-twenty in the morning. A Guardia Civil helicopter crosses the pale sky looking for god knows what. Seagulls. Dragonflies. The acid glow of the last neon lights from the hotels until, any moment now, out comes the Spanish sun.

Michela and Oliver are waiting in the car at the motorway exit, looking at the palm trees, forty of them, packed tight against their will on the roundabout, on the road to Barcelona. At this time of day, it's deserted. Oliver is looking east, towards the beach; the hotel signs have all just gone off at the same time. He reads the neon signs from the back, as if that was the important side, the side where everything happened and where luck always landed. As if everything turned its back on the front and it never mattered at all. Oliver is lying on the back seat, watching a video compilation on his phone, YouTube clips of how holding a gun in the movies has changed over the years: from the hip, with the arm straight out, palm down. He's taking all of this so literally; the kidnap, the stakeouts, the ransom demand all seem so real that they've taken him to a whole new dimension. He's going to give himself an alias. That's right, an alias.

"Why don't we play something," says Oliver, who's now bored after half an hour of videos. "There's still ages."

"We're already playing."

A man in bermudas is opening the shutters of a bar, a no-name bar, Bar Pepe or something, squashed under the weight of twenty-five storeys of electric-blue cement. The man looks at Michela. He lights a cigarette. It's half-six.

THE COP IN THE WOODS

I like woods
I like science
Detritus of millennia on the heads of millionaires,
    no need to walk
in a straight line
The trees, their clothing
The arm I found on my right
Cold works
Swamp
Wearing wet clothes, the smell of piss
Voices racing above my head

Michela has written this all in one go with red biro on the parking ticket pad. She reads it and rips it up.

"You talk less and less. You're quieter than ever," Oliver says to her. "What's up with you?"

"I speak less and less because I know more and more."

"Fuck, man. So Clint Eastwood."

"Clint Eastwood's a wuss."

But this isn't true. The only thing she knows for sure right now is that she's got to save her arse, her gym-trained arse, her Latina, three-dimples-per-buttock arse, and the only way to do that is to give up on the lighter. Release Anton somewhere very public and forget the lighter. It's her only way out.

Just at that moment, the Mercadona delivery van pulls calmly up to the traffic light.

"Oliver," says Michela. "This is it. Run."

Oliver opens the door, gets out of the car, charges to the middle of the roundabout and waves at the van driver to stop.

"What's going on!" The driver is Peruvian, very young. He's driving half off his face.

"I've got a flat battery," Oliver shouts.

The Peruvian says something under his breath and swerves the van to one side of the road. He gets out. The two of them come towards the car. Michela gets out and the Peruvian stops dead in his tracks when he sees her because he's come across her before, she's arrested him more than once. He knows the score.

"Chill," she says, smiling. Michela's smile makes him feel anything but chill.

"It's just a message," says Oliver.

"Fuck me," the Peruvian murmurs, arms crossed across his chest, eyes out on stalks.

Michela suddenly sees the glowing blue lights of a patrol car coming along the road. They have to be quick. She takes out an envelope and puts it in the Peruvian's shirt pocket.

"Put this in Kaminski's order."

"The one in the big house?"

The patrol car comes round the bend.

"The one in the big house. Quick. Get on with it."

"That's it?"

"Don't say anything," says Oliver. "Or I'll break your legs." He's been longing to say that.

"That's okay."

"Come on," says Michela. "Move it."

The Peruvian takes the envelope. There's a note inside.

ANTON LOBBY HOTEL BALI THURS 12.00

The Peruvian gets back in his van. Starts the engine. Leaves. Michela waves at her two colleagues; they're driving slowly, happy newbies, so fresh-faced. They're smiling. They ask her if something's happened. A breakdown, but it's sorted, she says. The newbies stop the car and get out. The four of them chat for a while on the hard shoulder about the previous day's match, Madrid–Barça. The smell of the first coffee of the day, news on the radio. Today is going to be a spectacular day.

215, 216, 217. Eleven at night, three rooms, one cheap hotel on the fifth block back from the beach, inset lighting, gold carpet, that sort of thing. Michela and Vilches are in the middle room, 216. In 215, there are three wheeler-dealer Catalans. In 217, it doesn't look like there's anybody. Yet. Michela and Vilches have been locked in 216 for six hours; this morning they hid a microphone and a camera in the smoke detector in 215 and now they're in the dark, not making a sound, each of them sitting on a bed covered in empty crisp packets. The three Catalans in 215 on the other hand are talking non-stop, in Catalan, so everyone knows exactly what they're on about. They've already had five lines each, Michela and Vilches can see on the screen at the end of the bed in 216 that's glimmering like a camp-fire, a talking campfire. One of the Catalans isn't Catalan, he's Andalucian from Seville, and speaks with an accent that Vilches finds hilarious. He doesn't laugh, but Michela knows him. The real Catalans and the fake one are sharing out five lots of developable land each the size of six football pitches, they've laid out a map of Benidorm on the floor and are kneeling, measuring out the property, its extent, and its boundaries like field marshals; they're going to put a river here, a ski slope there. More white powder.

"And another airport," says the Andalucian.

Michela and Vilches already have enough evidence to go into 215 and pick the three of them up, but they want to see how this plays out, see when the briefcase with the money appears, the briefcase with the dough, the dosh, the be-all and end-all of everything.

"And a casino on a boat," says one of them.

"We've not said anything about boats here."

"A floating casino. Do you get me?"

"I do."

"I don't."

"We've been looking for plots of land for donkey's years, as if terra firma was the only thing we could develop."

The guy from Seville puts his hands on his head because he suddenly gets it.

"Oh Christ."

"Nobody has ever tried to develop the sea."

Suddenly, in 217, which everyone thought was empty, the TV comes on at full volume.

"Fuck," says one of the Catalans.

It's a local programme: the singing children of Benidorm, the Thursday night choir competition.

"God, that TV," shouts the Andalucian.

Michela is going to thump the wall so that they turn the volume down, but she thinks it's better if everyone thinks 216 is empty.

"And bollocks to all that coastal regulation bollocks," says the Catalan from the city council. He isn't really Catalan either, Michela saw him a while ago getting out of his taxi to pay the driver. That means another Englishman, another fake Catalan.

"This is the start of something momentous," says the real Catalan.

"What did he say?" the man from Seville asks the Englishman.

"That we're going to make history with a capital H."

Suddenly a woman's voice starts singing in 217. A soft, deep, buttery sound like a blues singer.

"What's up?" Vilches whispers.

"Nothing," Michela replies.

It's not a famous song, but it sounds like seventies pop with a hint of jazz to it.

"You look upset all of a sudden."

The song is about a girl and her boyfriend, riding their motorbike along an endless road.

"I'm absolutely fine," says Michela.

But it's true, she's gone white as a sheet. Even in the gloomy hotel room, you can tell. The voice on the TV is her mother's voice. Laurana's voice, Laurana's thinly veiled voice. That voice that she gave a different name to every day: Bárbara, Carmela, Asunción, out of sheer boredom, the voice that she kept for singing in the club and nothing else, the voice that didn't even say goodbye before she left forever.

"Will those fuckers turn down that fucking TV," says one of the Catalans.

"I'll tell the bastards," says the man from Seville. He gets up and opens the door. Michela hears him go out into the corridor, go past 216, and immediately bang on the door of 217. "Turn it down," he screams.

In 217, nobody replies. Just the voice on the TV, that Eurovision 1975 voice.

He bangs again.

No answer.

Swearing under his breath, the man from Seville goes back to 215, where the other two are now so high that they've rung for three call girls to join the party. They crack open another bottle of Larios. They must be about to close the deal.

"To green shoots!" says the Englishman.

"Say cheese," murmurs Vilches, watching the Englishman getting the briefcase from under the bed on the monitor and pushing it with his foot towards the Catalan. The Catalan opens it.

Vilches springs to his feet and gestures to Michela. They get their handcuffs ready and go to the door, and in the instant before they leave, just out of the corner of her eye, for no more than a second, Michela sees the reflection of room 217 in the window of the building opposite, the light from the bathroom, the gleaming floor, the perfectly made bed, her father, Kyle, it's definitely him, sitting on it, staring at the gold carpeted floor, smoking, barefoot, in suit trousers and nothing else, thick-rimmed glasses, listening to Laurana's voice booming through the whole hotel, Michela and Viches then kick in the door to 215 and charge in and from then on everything happens super-fast, like something they've rehearsed a thousand times, and the Catalans are so gobsmacked they practically let them put the handcuffs on.

"Bollocks," says one. "This is a shit film."

The man from Seville starts to laugh, a demented *Friday the 13th* laugh, then he cries, and his sobbing follows them out into the corridor, where the one from the city council slips and falls on his knees. Michela picks him up by his shirt collar and pushes him downstairs to the cheap hotel lobby, aquamarine marble, dwarf palm, and the patrol cars, which are waiting with their doors open, because they deserve nothing less.

Half an hour later, when Michela comes back to the hotel from the main police station, 217 is completely dark. Empty. Kyle, her father, has already gone.

The Mini can be seen from more than two hundred metres away, the inside light is on, it looks like a little stage, lit up on the other side of the enormous wasteland behind the bus station car park, a chapel in a dark cathedral. Pine trees as a backdrop. Martin is inside the Mini, he borrows it from someone who comes to Benidorm now and then, he's playing electric guitar alone. The place is so far from where anybody lives that nobody can hear him, that's what he tells Michela. At that moment, two in the morning, Michela has arrived on her motorbike and has parked in the development down the road so that Martin won't see her. She walks towards the Mini, leaving a couple behind her who are screaming at each other because they've forgotten where they left the car; by the looks of things, they've been searching for a while and seem keener on screaming at each other than finding it, set to carry on searching for it for the rest of the night, for the rest of their lives.

Martin is sitting in the back seat of the Mini, in swimming trunks, doors open, four or five moths, flies, lazy insects attracted by the light. The car acts as a soundbox, so the music thunders as Michela gets nearer, and the guitar that she gave him as a present, that she'd picked up for a steal on eBay like some spare part, sounds better than she expected.

Slowly Michela crosses the wasteland, then she stops and looks at Martin, looks at him from a distance, she just wants to know what's going on, why it's been days since they've seen each other, why he's not picking up the phone. Martin is playing *The Wire*, the thing he whistles or sings or plays after a fuck, apparently this time not with her. She wants to know who with. Martin stops playing, as if he's sensed someone's there. Michela doesn't move a muscle. Now in the silence, there's just the night chirping of the cicadas, cicadas deep in the hot grass, cicadas above the trees, in the air, in stereo.

Martin is playing with Foneda Cox in one of the car parks at the Hotel Fenicia, the vast, closed-off pile in the middle of the city, the hotel that never opened and has been sitting there for thirty years, huge, looming, looking half-submerged, the floating tip of Benidorm's real-life dark web. When they started, there were five members of Foneda Cox, then three, and now four of them. The only one who was there the whole time was Martin, practising on a Kashmir carpet at the back of a garage that stank of Chinese food and dry piss. There are about forty people in the audience, with forever Friday night faces, Benidorm Friday night faces. Michela found out about the concert by chance, she saw it on one of the hundreds of flyers stuck to the lamp posts on the promenade. He hadn't told her anything about it. It's been days since she's had any sign of life from him, since he answered her calls. As well as the concert, there's an exhibition of a Valencian photographer who's printed out photos of the Benidorm skyscrapers in vertical tiles and put them all together in a row, so they look like the Playa Poniente skyline. The photographer is wandering about, taking photos with flash. Michela gets out of his way, she doesn't want to be in any photos, she doesn't really want Martin to see her, she wants to know why he hasn't told her about the concert and what's going on between them, because it's starting to piss her off, so she's checking out what's happening from a shadowy corner of the car park. Thirty metres away from everything.

She scans the place. She's not surprised to find the girl from Madrid there, the one from the other day, from the party, Kaminski's girlfriend. She's found out that she's a Torlonia, seventh generation, one of the Spanish branch of the Torlonias, a spin-off from the family tree who's ended up as a Zara model slash conceptual artist. Today the girl from Madrid is in a blue boiler suit and a pair of snakeskin boots. This morning, whilst she was on patrol, Michela saw her coming out of Gum. The hardcore of contemporary Benidorm is so contemporary that hardly any of the locals know about it, but half of Europe is there, like they were in the nineties with all the Ruta del Bacalao clubbing. The Spanish Levant, always at the cutting edge of the Occident, a cutting edge that wavers between excessive and extra-terrestrial with demented goings-on, like covering the Plaza Mayor of Valencia with slices of jamón serrano – that was cool – or setting fire to everything in sight, the giant figures from the Fallas, rice fields, dead girls, Nino Bravo in a purple tux singing into his mike in front of the Albufera in flames. The hardcore of contemporary Benidorm is Gum, a multidisciplinary creative hub. Which says it all. Behind the shopfront, there are three tattoo studios, an exhibition space, and a pop-up store with designer gear created by the place's owners, Romino and Angus, two local gays, Benidorm gays, who first met in primary school when they spent their Sunday pocket money sharing a taxi to take them to school every day, because those two on the school bus, no freaking way, bitch. The bestselling piece is a white tee with a big coffee stain in the middle. It goes for eighty euros. There's nothing else for under a hundred. When Michela saw the girl from Madrid coming out of there this morning, she had no handbag, nothing, she looked like she was going out for a fag, like she lived there, in the back of the shop.

Now the girl from Madrid is sitting on top of a TV monitor, old-school, cathode-ray, placed on the floor in a circle with six others in a video installation, super seventies. On the screens, low-quality black-and-white videos: CCTV videos of people stealing, pinching stuff in supermarkets and lingerie shops or in Tiger. Doing it without a care in the world, like real thieves, as if they know they're invisible, which they kind of are. The girl from Madrid is talking a couple through how she stole the videos, and the concept of appropriating the appropriated and the concept of plagiarism in culture, and it all sounds like Madrid-girl spoilt-brat shit to Michela. She carries on to the back of the space, undercover in contemporary Benidorm. When the video installation couple leave, the girl from Madrid sits back down on top of a TV, bored, takes out her phone, yawns like a proper artist. She starts whistling the theme tune to *The Wire*.

She goes to Gum. At Gum, Romino and Angus are in full photo-shoot swing for the new season. They're playing something by Blondie. Blondie would have been so Gum. When Romino and Angus see her come in, they ask her to pose, she's in uniform, they always ask her to pose when she's in uniform and she always says the same thing, no. At the back of the shop, there's a room for the artists-in-residence. That's what Romino calls them. It's also a storeroom for photos, a storeroom for clothes and for tabs and pills. Michela couldn't care less about all that. She's just come to confirm what she thinks she's got a sniff of. In the back of the shop, there's a shower behind a diamond-patterned curtain, and next to it a purple velvet three-seater sofa with a pillow and sheet chucked on top. Boxes, envelopes, bottles. Michela sits down. She scans the place. Debbie Harry is still singing about hearts of glass on the stereo. On the table, there's a tin of Amsterdamer, a Fujifilm X70, the September issue of *Vogue Italia*, a ring that she knows belongs to the girl from Madrid, she's seen it in photos. On the back of a chair, she spots Martin's yellow Mr E T-shirt. She picks it up. It's sweaty, limp like an old banknote. The tattoo artist's machine is buzzing outside, and Blondie, and nothing else.

When she gets up to leave after ten long minutes thoroughly planning her next move and its consequences, she discovers a glass with a toothbrush and tube of toothpaste on a red plastic chair. Next to the glass is Reggie Kray's gold lighter.

When Michela opens the door with a credit card, Gizmo and Fernando are sitting waiting in the middle of Kyle's hall. The flat is dark; Michela wonders what dogs do in empty houses at night when there's nobody there. They're very calm, they don't bark, they don't move from where they're sitting. In the flat above, they're having a party; weirdly you can't hear a note of music, but the ceiling is rumbling with the weight of people dancing, and the pieces of the plastic rock crystal chandelier are rattling violently above the hall table with its five copies of *The Guardian*, unopened, and an empty bottle of Macallan. She scans the place. She doesn't want to turn on the light: light and silence make bad bedfellows. Silence and darkness suit each other, even more so if you throw in heat as well. She goes to the bathroom. Operating theatre green. She sees splatters of toothpaste on the mirror, as if Kyle had got too close when he was brushing, as if he was searching for something there in the mirror, something in his big, wide face, but looking for what. Or whom.

She doesn't know where to leave the lighter. On the stairs before she came in, she spent a while looking at it in the palm of her hand. Michela wonders whether the girl from Madrid has a clue about the value of this object that's so mythical, so iconic to her, whether Kaminski has given it to her as some grand gesture, but Michela doesn't think Russians make grand gestures unless they're pissed. The girl probably picked it up one day, on the off chance, not a second thought, and has forgotten to give it back. The lighter is a long, fluted Dunhill, gold-plated like Miss Benidorm's cheap diamanté crown. It's heavy and it's elegant and for a minute Michela thinks it should be in a display case in a museum.

She goes out onto the terrace. The wicker sofa takes up nearly all the space. It's round, like the one in the *Emmanuelle* films. She sits down for a moment. The seat creaks like old bones. You can't see the sea from here, the only view is of the back sides of buildings, fire escapes, fluorescent lights flickering in kitchens, a hundred thousand air conditioning units. On the table, there's a box of Camels next to a yellow plastic Bic lighter and a pile of unwashed dishes. A pillbox with big pills that look like vitamins and tiny ones that look properly scary. Someone on the floor above starts watering the plants on their terrace, the jet gushing past before splashing down twelve floors below.

Michela picks up the Bic. She leaves Reggie's lighter there on the table next to the dirty dishes.

When she leaves, the dogs don't move, in fact they haven't moved this whole time, they've just stared at her from the door. They weren't waiting for her; not for a second.

Here, Michela is nobody. They're waiting for Kyle.

A triumphal entrance means nothing. What matters is the exit, the ending, the placing of the final full stop, so that when you leave, the party's over, the lights come back on, and the rubbish gets taken out. So that everyone leaves the way they came, in the lift of a skyscraper under construction. The lift goes up, suspended in the void, rising very slowly on the exterior of the façade that still isn't a façade, no walls, just thousands of square metres of air on a reinforced concrete floor. On the twentieth floor of forty-two, they pass through a strong gust of wind, as if they enter a different state of reality every ten floors. Vilches doesn't like heights; with his chin stuck to his chest, he's clinging on to the handrail and staring out at the horizon, which isn't there because it's three in the morning.

Michela turns on her phone again. She's got seven messages from Oliver. She ran into him before lunch in the street with all the Basque pintxo bars; he must have been waiting for her, because he knows that Michela goes to the same bar for a couple of vermouths every day at the same time, one-thirty. He was sitting at the bar, looking at the door when she got there. He smiled at her from under the hood of his fuchsia sweatshirt that was pulled down round his eyebrows, biting the skin round his thumbnail. He had a look about him.

Michela goes up to him and stops six inches from his face. "What?"

Oliver hesitates for a moment; he's obviously prepared something more complex to say than he usually does, something that was working really well in his head, but now he doesn't know where to begin.

"Right."

He's more nervous than pissed off. Without shifting her stare from Oliver's face, Michela raises a finger at the waiter to order her usual. Then she moves away and sits down. Bored.

"You've not picked up all day," says Oliver.

"I'm working."

"I'm working too."

"Yeah, but I'm a police officer."

The bar is very noisy, laughter, bad jokes, Basques, the Andalucians of the north. Michela listens in on the conversations, next to the toilets they're talking about money, she can tell, they've lowered their voices, in Spain when you speak about money you either lower your voice or every man and his dog finds out. Michela isn't interested in cash, in money itself. Michela is interested in information about where money can be found. She knows full well that real fortunes belong to people who have never seen a euro coin, even from a distance, and that the higher up you are in the pyramid of laundering dirty money, the less you get to touch it.

"How much am I going to get for this operation?" Oliver blurts out.

Michela bursts out laughing.

"Plastic surgeon now, are you?"

"No. I'm sitting here now. And now you're going to listen to me."

His voice has suddenly changed. That sounded like somebody who's made sure they know the way out before they come in. Michela's guard goes up.

"This is not the place," she says.

"I don't care."

"Do you want a boat?"

They have a lot of confiscated boats, flats, many-cylinder-engine motorbikes, fine jewels.

"A boat. What the fuck do I want a boat for?"

"It won't be for much longer."

"You mess me around the whole time, don't you?"

"Look. Let's meet this evening. Somewhere different."

"No. Now."

"And we'll sort it. You have my word."

"Where? When? It's all words with you, isn't it, and they don't mean much."

"I'm on duty. I'll let you know."

Michela gets down from her stool. She knocks the vermouth back in one and goes towards the door.

"Michela," Oliver shouts after her.

But Michela doesn't turn round. Nor does she answer his messages or calls for the rest of the afternoon. The last one was five hours ago.

When they get to the forty-second floor, the top floor, the lift shakes to a halt. Michela and Vilches jump out.

The cement floor is shaking with the bass from Foneda Cox, who are playing in the middle of the thousand-square-metre space, surrounded on four sides by air and the Mediterranean night. They've put some LED spotlights between the twenty or thirty of their mates who make up the audience. Some are dancing, others are drunk, others are lying around on the floor, completely shit-faced. Foneda Cox are playing "Gimme Hunger". It all sounds terrible.

When Vilches blows his whistle, the music carries on as if nothing's happening.

"They can't hear," says Michela.

Vilches whistles again several times as they push their way through the crowd towards the band. Three girls start dancing with Vilches; they think he's hilarious, like a big bear. Michela swats them away and they press on. When the band eventually hear the whistle and see two police officers coming towards them with their arms in the air, they suddenly stop. Michela has got her truncheon out too. Martin wrinkles his brow. He looks out of it.

"Licence," Vilches says to the drummer, who's the tallest and always looks like the one in control. "You have got a licence to play here, right? Are you charging admission? And the emergency exit, where is it? You and you, stay exactly where you are."

The drummer looks at Vilches, then at Michela, then back at Vilches. He bursts out laughing.

"What are you laughing at?" says Vilches.

"I'm scared. Of what's going to happen."

"Fucking buzzkill," shouts a girl, somewhere behind them.

Martin snaps out of it and looks at Michela like he doesn't understand what's going on.

"Licence," is all that Michela says. She's got his yellow Mr E T-shirt that he left at Gum after hanging out with the girl from Madrid. Martin sees it and closes his eyes. "Shit," he whispers.

"ID."

"Can we talk?" he asks Michela.

"Down at the station," Michela replies. "Now, ID."

Martin takes out his identity card. He hands it to Michela, who doesn't touch it.

"For my colleague."

Martin gives his ID to Vilches, and the other band members – apart from the drummer, who is completely off his face – just hand over their identity cards with the odd expletive and yawn. They're used to it. Whatever.

"Come with me," says Vilches.

"Now?" asks the drummer, who can't stand up.

"Everyone out," says Michela.

"What about this one?"

"He stays here."

They leave all their music gear where it is on the floor and Vilches starts pushing them towards the staircases. Martin turns round to look at Michela, standing there with her arms folded. She doesn't move. She's made sure that he won't be playing again for a while, that he'll end up spending a few months in the slammer. She's slipped a bag of pills into the back pocket of his jeans without him realising; he's got no clue what's waiting for him when they search him at the police station.

"Get on with it. Fucking go home," shouts Vilches.

The audience breaks up, they don't even moan that much, they weren't even that good, it's not even like it's a big deal. That's the youth of today. A group of them go down in the lift, others down the fire escape. After a few minutes there's hardly anyone left. A girl of about fourteen, who keeps throwing up, ends up being carried by her three friends down the staircase that's still under construction. Michela hears them laughing until they stop a few floors down, where they'll sleep it all off until midday tomorrow.

Deserted. Michela turns off the LED spotlights. She wanders through the space in the half-light, alone, like a medieval queen in an empty castle. She grabs her phone and texts Oliver.

Floor 42 of the Paradiso.

She sends it.

She waits a few seconds.

Read.

She gets an answer straight back.

I'll be there in ten.

She's planning to give him ten big ones, she's got them with her, it's more than she thought at the beginning, but she knows that without Oliver the whole thing wouldn't have turned out as well as it did. And besides, she likes him.

Michela goes up to the edge of the building. A few hours ago, before it got dark, there were big storm clouds gathering; clouds as thick as swamp water, to disappear into, searching for ghosts; heavy, yellow clouds. But the storm never came, the clouds have kept their downpour somewhere inside and are sweating it out like a fever, leaving a liquid sky, a damp glow that makes everything wet. A sky that smells good, a sky like seaweed.

Michela takes a step nearer to the edge of the building. She looks at the sea, the reflections of the skyscrapers' lights on the water, red and yellow strips, vertical like standards, an army waiting for the bellow of the hunting horn.

She can't hear a thing. The wind. Something murmuring just for her, that only she can hear.

She moves towards the stairs. She stops when she hears the noise of the lift coming up the façade. The lift stops dead. Michela sees the three of them. They're walking slowly towards her, all in step. Oliver between Anton and Kaminski, like a fortress wall, three compact silhouettes, three perfect, solid, silent shadows.

Kaminski is carrying a pistol. Anton is carrying a pistol.

Oliver is carrying a pistol as well.

Michela's shadow fell right in the middle of the travel agent's window, between the reflections of the hundreds of skyscrapers behind her, the traffic lights, and the kilometres of palm trees, bent like elastic, frazzled by the sun. It was August, it was summer. It was summer every day of the year.

"Michela!"

Michela took out her little camera and snapped a photo of a country, England. Her nails were painted orange, it was the first time in her life that she'd painted her nails, just like it was the first time she'd seen a poster of England, or anything like it. She was nine.

"Michela!"

Kyle was calling her from the other side of the road. He was in lace-up shoes, stripy trousers, a thin tie, black. Michela went over to her father, scraping her enormous flip-flops, Kyle's flip-flops, on the ground, crossing the street without looking. Behind her father, a kiosk with a poster for the première of *The Goonies* and another saying "Gold Bought Here".

"Don't go to sleep on the job."

Kyle put his hands in the back pockets of his trousers. He looked out towards the main avenue with its stalls and karaoke bars and motorbikes and headed off in that direction.

He walked slowly, striding out, covering a lot of ground quickly.

They left one overgrown, vacant plot of land, one of the city's thousands of future funeral pyres, and came to another, where the ground was covered in broken tiles and building rubble and where there was a red armchair under a mountain pine, surrounded by sunflower seed shells. They crossed to the other pavement and got to the avenue with its traffic, people on their way back from the beach, cooked Germans and smoked Dutch women, pensioners, Russians, the shops were already shut but the market stalls were still going. That year the summer drink was a huge plastic litre bottle of something blue with a ton of alcohol and even more sugar, and all the tourists were carrying it around with them, letting it get warm.

Around the corner, a bit further on, they almost bumped into a woman looking at a jacaranda. In blossom. Jacarandas are always enormous, showy, shop window kind of trees, and the woman was staring at it like it was something unexpected in a city like this, staring at its fragile, elegant, sadly try-hard exoticism in a city like this, and she wasn't wrong. She was standing there, distracted. Kyle looked at her. Then he turned his head and beamed a glowing smile in Michela's direction. All teeth. Kyle raised one, two, three fingers. Michela shrugged her shoulders then nodded. She frowned. Kyle pointed with his head to one of the alleys that led down towards the beach and started walking slowly in that direction. Michela went up to the woman. From behind.

She wiped her sweaty palms on her T-shirt. She stopped. She slipped her hand into the woman's bag. She took out her wallet. At that moment, there were about forty people less than ten metres away, but nobody saw her putting the wallet inside her T-shirt, or nobody wanted to see, which amounts to the same thing, and she started running towards the beach. The woman said something in English. She screamed. Three or four tourists turned to look, but their sunstroke slash hangover slash tiredness got the better of them. Michela ran down the slope, not in a particular hurry, reluctantly almost, occasionally looking behind her. Then she carried on walking, dragging those flip-flops behind her. When she arrived at the promenade, she looked around for Kyle. He was on the shore, in a Zodiac. She saw him take out his Swiss army knife and cut the mooring. Michela walked slowly along the shore. She jumped into the Zodiac, dumped the woman's wallet on the seat. Kyle started the engine.

Out to sea. More sea.

Further out.

Nostalgia for empires. Nostalgia for empires and continents, for naval battles, for Trafalgar. Nostalgia for journeys across oceans guided only by maps of the currents fashioned from the threads of an English officer's uniform, knots representing islands and archipelagos, red strands intertwining on a balsa wood stretcher hanging next to a picture of Reggie and Ronnie and a postcard from Manchester pinned to the wall. English melancholy, fierce, factual, remorseless, so different from our own. Under the map, a pile of books: Hitchens, David Peace, the complete set of *Just William* books, bought for only a pound. The King James Bible.

Gizmo and Fernando are still sitting in the same spot in front of the door when Kyle comes in. They don't move, they know Kyle doesn't like them to make a fuss, to run around, to jump up, to bark. He's an Englishman. A very tall Englishman who in his youth used to stand with his legs slightly apart so he'd be the same height as everyone else. Now he just goes around with his back hunched and his head down, with wiry white hair and a five-day beard on his long face. With eyebrows like a couple of stitches. He leaves the light off and drops his keys on the bed. He opens the fridge, which is in the sitting room, and shuts it again without taking anything out. He kicks off his trainers with his heels and slips off onto the terrace barefoot, like someone in an insurance ad. Still a handsome Englishman. Gizmo and Fernando are at either side of the upright wooden chair with its wicker seat. Kyle sits down and picks up the packet of cigarettes, leans back, and rests a bare foot on the edge of the table. He looks at the vertical horizon of the building opposite, the sky high above with clouds scattered strangely like spelling mistakes. Then he sees the lighter. Golden, long, narrow. Like him. He knows exactly what he's looking at but does nothing. Not a thing. He looks at it for a good while without blinking, without touching it. He sighs. Gizmo and Fernando yawn at the same time. Kyle sits up. He picks up the lighter. Smooth. It was smooth. It is smooth. He turns it around and looks at it from both sides. He lifts it up to his forehead to check its temperature. It's cold. He strokes its fluted surface slowly with his thumb, as if he was rubbing a lamp to summon up Reggie's spirit, his Elizabethan ghost, his thuggish ghost, his ghost from a past that never was, and with it, all the ghosts.

Kyle lights a cigarette. He lights a cigarette with the lighter that isn't even gold, but plate, that isn't genuine, but looks like it should be. Gizmo and Fernando get up, they go inside, into the dark. Kyle takes a first, long drag. The cigarette lights like it would with any other lighter, tastes like any other cigarette, burns like cigarettes always burn. It burns like a fiver or a five-hundred-euro note, burns like broken flags, like lances, like galleons, burns like trees, like the wood that begins to move, like the battle upon St Crispin's Day. It burns like everything burns, until all that's left is smoke and air and nothing.

Foundry Editions
40 Randolph Street
London NW1 0SR
United Kingdom

First published in 2022 as *Spanish Beauty* by Editorial Anagrama, S.A., Barcelona

This first edition published by Foundry Editions in 2025

The moral right of Esther García Llovet to be identified as the Author of this work has been asserted in accordance with the Copyright, Designs and Patents Act 1988.

A CIP record for this title is available from the British Library.

ISBN 978-1-7384463-8-4

Series cover design by Murmurs Design
Designed and typeset in LfA Aluminia by Tetragon, London
ARC Printed and bound by CPI Group (UK) Ltd

foundryeditions.co.uk

KARIM KATTAN

The Palace on the Higher Hill

Translation by Jeffrey Zuckerman

PALESTINE

Faysal, a young Palestinian man in exile, gets a mysterious letter about the death of an aunt he can't remember. He leaves his life in Europe behind and returns to Palestine, to the village of his birth and his extraordinary, deserted family house, the Palace on the Higher Hill. As he roams its once glorious rooms and the threat of occupation gets ever nearer, voices from the past return to shed light on his own family's story and on the story of his people.

Through its beautifully written story and unforgettable cast of characters, who occupy a dizzying space between the imaginary and the real, *The Palace on the Higher Hill* gives a nuanced, human, and deeply moving panorama of the tragedy of conflict and brings English-speaking readers an unexpected, furious vision of Palestine that feels entirely new.

The Palace on the Higher Hill won the 2021 Prix des Cinq Continents de la Francophonie.

ANNA PAZOS

Killing the Nerve

Translation by Laura McGloughlin and Charlotte Coombe

SPAIN/CATALONIA

Not so much autofiction as autojournalism, *Killing the Nerve* dissects the end of youth and the beginning of adulthood for the global nomad generation. Fleeing the 'Mediterranean mediocrity' of bourgeois Barcelona life, Anna Pazos's story hurtles us from wasted Erasmus days in Thessaloniki, through a period in Jerusalem, and a voyage across the Atlantic with an unsuitable lover to post-MeToo New York.

When she is forced back to Barcelona with the pandemic, she turns her super-cool scalpel-like eye and super-intelligent, incisive language on her family within the context of Catalan society, especially the independentist movement, and on her place in that world.

This stunning debut has been a hit at home. It was longlisted for the Premi Finestres 2023 and voted Best Catalan Book of the Year by "Babelia", *El Pais*' prestigious cultural supplement.

**FOUNDRY
EDITIONS**